I0593603

A
SINGLE
SNOW

A Destarny Novel

First published in Australia in May 2023 by KDP publishing

Text copyright © Destarny 2023

A catalogue record for this book is available from the National Library of Australia

ISBN 978-0-6457366-0-1 (paperback)
ISBN 978-0-6457366-1-8 (ebook)

www.adestarnynovel.com

BY DESTARNY

A SINGLE SNOW

To my sister who cried

A SINGLE SNOW

Destarny

PROLOGUE

I opened my eyes. The sunlight reached the bottom of the ocean, illuminating the murky water. I slowly sat up and looked at Arnold, who was kneeling next to me.

"Layla, it's time to head home."

I nodded and he stood. His blue hair and eyes changed to black hair and eyes as he reverted to his human form. His transformation complete, he left the water.

I rubbed my eyes. It had been another challenging night. At this pace, maybe Arnold would be able to handle a third of the workload himself by the end of this year.

He was finally able to make half of the winter weather using the powers I had given him. He was doing very well. But we only had a year left…

A tornado of water swirled around me. At the signal, I stood up and walked towards the shore.

No. I have to push him harder. He needs to do better than that. It won't be enough. Especially when we're low in numbers.

I got out of the water and quickly grabbed the towel from Arnold's hands, pulling it over my head so my face would be covered. My long wavy blue hair turned its usual human black within a second.

Holding onto the towel, I dusted the sand off my dry dress and turned to look at the ocean. It was always beautiful in the morning… it gave me hope that there would be a bright new day to come. We headed towards the car, turning our backs on the sun.

CHAPTER ONE

"Layla, breakfast is ready," Arnold called out. From his voice, I could tell he was still upset.

I stopped working and waved a hand over the paperwork the Ministers had given me; it disappeared. I left my bedroom and headed to the dining room. Arnold was sitting at the table looking down like I knew he would be.

"The Ministers spoke badly of you, as usual," I said. "Just ignore them, like I do." I sat across from him.

He looked at me then. "You're a Queen. Of course you can ignore them. I'm just a servant. How am I allowed to ignore them?"

Queen? What kind of Queen was as powerless as me?

"To me you're not a servant, and you know that. You're my personal bodyguard now. If any one of them wants to argue with me, then they can write a formal complaint."

"Layla is completely right, sweetie!" Maria yelled. She was in the kitchen preparing our breakfast.

"Even your mother agrees with me," I said. "For the past four years, the Ministers have been trying to demote you. I'm tired of listening to them, aren't you?"

He gave me a long face, but I pretended not to notice.

"Hey now, that's not true," Maria said as she carried in our plates, the food hidden under a cover. "They always find a new reason to blame you. What did they complain about this time?"

"Yesterday I made the hallway *slightly* foggy, and they said Arnold must have been the cause and that is why he shouldn't be my bodyguard anymore."

"Those Ministers really have nothing better to say. They're just jealous of you, darling," Maria said, lowering the plates in front of us.

I could tell that Arnold was slowly losing his calm. "But they were right. What if you hadn't been able to see where you were going and tripped over and hurt yourself? What if your identity had been exposed?"

"But none of that happened because the air conditioners were on. The fog disappeared in less than a second. No one even noticed," I said, pouring a cup of water for him.

Arnold jumped up. "It was still a second! *Anything* could have happened. You could have–"

That was when he accidentally knocked the cup out of my hands. The water spilled all over my arm. The moment the water touched my skin, it turned into ice.

Many things happened at once. The curtains in the living room closed, drawn by the wind that Maria created, plunging the room into darkness. Arnold left the house saying, "I'll scout for any bystanders that might have seen."

I commanded the ice to turn back into water and it changed instantly. I stared at my wet arm. Only I had this problem. The human body couldn't contain the powers of the Winter Queen. So water would turn into ice every time I touched it. How I hated this life.

Maria glanced at my wet arm and used her wind again to open the curtains. A couple of minutes later, Arnold came back inside the house. "Sorry! I didn't mean to!"

"It's fine. See, all wet," I said.

It had taken me a long time to master the command in case we ever had any incidents at school. Before, it would have taken me a week to change it back to water. I'd come a long way. But we'd also created a routine to protect what we had now.

Maria went to the kitchen and came out with paper towels. "Arnold dear, you need to calm down," she said, helping me dry my arm. "The Ministers were picking on you. It's not your fault. Whose fault would it be?" The question was directed to me.

"Humans."

Maria expected further elaboration but she knew how I felt, so she didn't bother to ask. She turned to Arnold and ruffled his hair.

"Exactly. So don't be so hard on yourself, sweetie. Plus, she's safe now. We're all safe." Then she commanded the spilled water on the table to dry. It disappeared right away. "Let's all calm down and eat, shall we?"

I poured myself and Maria a cup and took a sip from the straw Maria gave me. Arnold was watching me. It seemed to calm him down since he didn't say anything else.

"Alright, my new recipe. Enjoy!" Maria took the covers off, revealing our plates. She kept turning her head to look at our faces. "What's wrong?"

It was normal for droplet cakes to come in all sorts of shapes and colours, but usually they were transparent. Not like the one in front of us, which had tiny, brown, unidentifiable cubes swimming in it.

"Maria, are you trying to poison us?" Arnold asked as he poked at his cake. I couldn't help but ask the same question.

"Yes, Maria… what are these brown cubes?" I took a scoop and examined them. Shockingly, they were still swimming around.

"Don't worry! They just make the cake extra crunchy."

Arnold and I looked at her in doubt. But she smiled brightly.

"Would you like me to spoon-feed you?"

The image of her coddling us like babies prompted us to eat our cakes. I took my first bite. The brown cubes indeed made the cake crunchier. How they were swimming in the cake, I did not want to ask. But it added more flavour, more coldness to the rest of the cake, which tasted like a raging storm inside. A wet, windy, thundering cake, which I had to admit was a nice added touch.

"Other than the Ministers, how was yesterday night?" Maria sat and took her first bite. Then she nodded at her cake. "I did a good job this time."

I smiled. "It was good. At this rate, Arnold will be able to handle all of the workload by himself."

"Why Arnold, you're doing so well! Soon Layla can just relax. Looks like you won't need to worry about winter weather-making anymore."

I nodded and took a bite.

"But when?" Arnold looked at me.

I could have lied to them. They wouldn't have known if I did. But I didn't want to lie. Not about this. And not to them.

"You only have a tenth of my powers, and you've been managing better than anyone else could have. We just need to work a bit harder. Tonight I'll give you a little more work. We'll see if you can handle it then."

Arnold went back to eating. "I will work harder. I won't disappoint you."

"Dear, you've done so much," Maria said. Arnold didn't say anything else.

Arnold had the most pressure on him out of all of us. He needed to master winter-making on his own. Once he becomes of age, we can take back the authority we had lost.

And he would become King of Winter.

We had to prepare for that day. I couldn't say anything to comfort him. Anything I said now would just become empty hopes until we'd achieved our goal.

Maria started telling funny stories from her meteorology workplace. That brought a smile to Arnold's face. Maria always had the power to cheer people up. I watched them talk as I ate.

I will protect these two people, whom are the most precious to me.

CHAPTER TWO

"AHHHHH!"

It was the first day back to school in Perth, a small city in Australia. And already, we had been welcomed with the sound of a scream as we entered the science hallway. Normally school would be empty at this early hour, but a lot of people were crowding around a locker. A girl was crouched on the floor, crying into her hands. More girls, presumably her friends, surrounded her, trying to comfort her, but slowly, one by one, they left.

Judging from the reaction, I had an idea of what had happened. The locker bore the mark of a flame, confirming my suspicions. The girl had become the latest victim of Brigid's gang.

Arnold touched my elbow.

Should we come back later? he asked through our touch.

We'll be safe. Don't worry, I answered.

We walked to our lockers, which were near the end of the hallway. The girls, who were her *friends*, were walking away, laughing at a joke – as if nothing had happened. The crying girl noticed this and cried harder.

I opened my locker. Humans. Such pathetic creatures. At the first sign of danger, they bolt faster than lightning. Leaving the weak ones behind. Cowards.

A gang of boys and girls stalked towards the crouching girl. Brigid's gang. And there was Brigid herself, her red wavy hair flowing. Everyone looked down as she walked past. For someone so short, she commanded a lot of fear. She reached the locker and stared down at the cowering girl, her arms folded, an expression of triumph in her amber eyes.

One of the gang members was holding a bin. Inside were scrunched-up scraps of paper. One by one the others reached in and threw them at her – as if *she* was the trash bin. The bits of paper had writing on them, and I had a fair idea of what they would say – nasty names and insults in every language.

Some of the scraps were larger and hit her hard as if they were wrapped around something... rocks. They were throwing rocks at her. She tried to cover herself, but it was no use. There were too many of them.

Cuts and scratches appeared on her skin. She begged them to stop, but they kept on going. She cried for help, but we all kept watching. Because that was what Brigid wanted. An audience.

The teachers walked by and said nothing. That was how much power Brigid had. Just because her parents funded and owned the school, everyone was afraid of her. No one dared to stand up to her.

The crying girl got up and made to run, but one of the members kicked her back down. They kept up the onslaught. She tried to block and looked around, her pleading eyes landing on mine. Either she realised who I was, or she saw the cold look I gave her. She slumped on the floor and curled in on herself. I took my books for my morning classes.

Yes that's right. I won't help you. Because you are weak. Humans are weak.

I closed my locker and looked at her curled body.

You're right not to expect anything from me. Or anyone. It was your fault you ended up like this. You're not doing anything for yourself but you expect others to help. I don't want to help someone who only relies on others.

I walked towards the end of the hallway, away from all the drama.

"I heard you didn't say nice things to my junior

here. Say it once more." Brigid's voice rang out loud and clear.

The only response was sobbing.

"I'm sorry, I didn't understand that. Try speaking in English." There were snickers around her. "Come on, say it once more you bi–"

I left the hallway before I could hear the rest and headed towards our homeroom. Brigid thought she was strong. But someone who needs to bully others to make themselves feel better is actually insecure. She was even weaker than the girl that was crying on the floor. Then why... I stopped and took a deep breath, then let it out.

How I hate humans.

"Layla, are you okay?"

I nodded in response to Arnold's question.

We walked into the classroom. Our teacher was reading. He saw us and gave a nod. I sat in the back corner while Arnold went to get a newsletter from the teacher's desk. We waited for the bell.

This was the privilege we got when we informed the school I was afraid of water. Just a medical note from my "psychologist" that I had aquaphobia was all I needed. Access to classes early and permission to leave early. Compulsory school events or classes I didn't need to attend. The advantages had worked out well for us because it helped lower the risk of my powers being revealed. But this was the only school that allowed these privileges.

After a few minutes, the bell rang. People from our homeroom slowly came in. I folded my arms and stared out at the sky, wishing time would fly faster.

"Year elevens, you have your first ball dance lessons after school today. You are required to attend if you want to go to the ball."

I tuned into what the homeroom teacher was saying. The other elevens in the room started buzzing. I turned to Arnold and we both smiled in anticipation.

"Layla, do you think we should attend?" he whispered.

"Did you forget this was your idea?" I whispered.

He remembered but still seemed concerned. The main reason we were attending was because Arnold and Maria wanted me to have a small break from everything. Even though I'd been dragged into it, I couldn't help but feel excited. I hadn't danced for so long.

"Okay, today we'll be teaching you the waltz."

The teachers showed us the moves for girls and boys at opposite ends of the gym. Some girls were struggling, while others were making fun of the whole thing. Especially Brigid and her girls. They kept laughing at every step, to the point I blocked them out.

I was in my own little world, going through the moves as I remembered them with ease. It's funny that even though our world is different from humans, the dances are all the same.

After an hour of the same moves, the teacher made us partner up. Arnold came up to me and offered his hand. I wanted to laugh but kept my face neutral. He could see the smile in my eyes though, and I could see his.

"You're all doing fine. Let's see how you can work with a partner. Alright, music start!"

While the others fumbled about, Arnold and I simply glided across the gym, our movements elegant and steps smooth. He spun me and I twirled. I nearly giggled. I'd forgotten how it felt to dance. I looked into Arnold's gleeful eyes. He knew how much I enjoyed it. No one took any notice of us. The focus was somewhere else.

"Ow!" a male voice cried nearby.

"I-I'm so sorry..." There were snickers around us.

That broke a little of the magic. I took a quick look. Brigid was waltzing around a couple, laughing. That meant a member of her gang was causing trouble this time.

The girl in the couple kept stepping on the boy's foot. But on closer inspection, it was no accident... He was making her step on him on purpose. Trying to make her look like she was the one who couldn't dance

– embarrassing her. And Brigid's gang knew that was why they were enjoying the show.

I glanced at the teachers. They were all distracted by different couples. But they were also purposely ignoring the commotion, as they always did.

"That's okay, I should be leading better. I'm just distracted by your beauty," said the boy.

I took another quick glance at the couple while Arnold steered me away from them. Seeing the girl's reaction, I understood what he was really trying to do. And the real reason why Brigid was laughing. They were trying to see how much he could charm her, despite him embarrassing her. And it was working. She blushed.

From then on, I ignored the gang and focused on dancing. I didn't want to ruin this moment. I didn't want to lose the feeling that dancing was giving me. For the longest time, I felt peaceful and content. It made me forget what lay ahead and let me enjoy the moment.

I remembered how much I'd disagreed in the beginning. I honestly thought it was a bad idea. But now, I was thankful that Arnold and Maria had convinced me. This was quite fun.

Thank you. I passed the message to Arnold through our connection.

He teared up a little, and I shook my head with a smile.

The teacher made us dance a few more rounds. No

one paid any attention to us. Everyone was happy.

Then the last dance came, and the teacher decided to give us a surprise.

"Okay. Let's change partners!"

Arnold and I tensed. Most of the class in the room protested.

"In that case, let's do it this way. Girls form a circle and boys make another circle around the girls."

We looked at each other. This was not supposed to happen. If I'd known this was going to happen, I would have argued to the end. I glared at Arnold. I'd warned him that something like this might happen. But then I softened my expression. Arnold looked like he might have a panic attack.

I didn't want to make a big deal and draw attention to us. I sighed and resigned myself to the situation. We should be fine. Even though I didn't want to touch a human. Arnold saw that I didn't do anything and followed suit. We all moved into place as the teacher had asked. Now there was an outer circle of boys and an inner circle of girls.

"Now boys, move to the left ten spaces and girls, move to the right ten spaces." We all did as we were told. "Okay, now these are your new dance partners for this last song."

The person in front of me looked familiar. But I

couldn't remember which class I'd seen him in. Brown hair... brown eyes... tall... muscular... A light bulb lit. That's right. He wasn't in any of my classes, he was the boy who had embarrassed the girl earlier. The one in Brigid's gang.

This couldn't get any worse.

One of his friends smirked as he walked past us.

"Oooh, a challenge Sasha."

This could get worse. I looked for Arnold. His expression told me everything I needed to know – he was ready to bolt and take me out of here. That meant the boy was who I thought he was.

I kept my face neutral as I faced him. I remembered a bit more now. Sasha Reynold... Brigid's favourite person. Now I couldn't pretend to be sick, even if I had planned to. I was locked down to be his next target. There was no way to escape.

"Hey, don't I know you?" he started. I shook my head like a little lost girl. "Yeah, you're the girl with the beautiful smile."

He even dared to wink at me.

I didn't say anything and glanced at the floor, pretending to be shy. But I cursed the world for this setup. When I looked up, Brigid's gang were hanging around us like sharks circling their prey.

Looks like I need to be in top condition. I'll need to give my best performance.

"Is everyone ready?" the teacher called out.

"May I have this dance?" He reached out his hand and I took it.

"Music cue!"

Then we started to move. He wasn't actually incapable of dancing. He just chose not to. He was watching me as I focused on the steps to keep myself calm. Brigid and her gang weren't always around us. Instead, they would take turns. That worked out better for me. As long as Brigid wasn't always around, this wouldn't be the worst. Everything would be fine as long as he didn't talk to me again.

"Don't we have a class together?" I looked up at him. Of course he would talk to me. I wouldn't be able to avoid that. "I could've sworn we had chemistry."

Do these lines actually work on girls? I wished the song would end soon. I gave him a shy smile.

"I-I'm sure it was arts... because a masterpiece like yourself wouldn't react to me."

His eyes shone brightly. He liked that answer. And glancing at Brigid, she liked what she was hearing too.

"A fine masterpiece *you* are," he said.

I looked away, embarrassed.

"I don't think it's chemistry or arts," he said.

I looked at him dreamily. "What class would we be in?"

"I want to be in a class where you're the one teaching."

If I was a human girl, I would have thrown up. This was really testing my emotions. But if I kept talking to him, maybe he wouldn't try anything else. As long as he didn't step on my foot, I could keep this appearance up. After all, the song was about halfway through, and Brigid was no longer near us. With that thought, it became more bearable. I could do this.

"What could you learn from me?"

"If it's about you, everything."

I wanted to freeze his mouth shut.

Suddenly he took a wrong step.

How dare he! I'll show him.

With a calm expression, I used his momentum, grabbed his hand and twirled myself. It was a perfect turn that would appear as if he were the one who'd led me into it. The teacher gasped as we danced near her. We got back in position and he looked surprised for a second, then smiled devilishly.

"So you can dance."

I didn't say anything, just showed him an innocent and confused look.

He wants to embarrass me? To show that he's such a good dancer and I'm the bad one? Who does he think he is? I refused to give in. My pride wouldn't allow me to.

I had kept my face free from any traces of my

thoughts, but he must have seen something in my eyes because he took a wrong step again. I changed our direction smoothly.

He tried again. I glanced at Brigid, who wasn't paying attention to us anymore – she was toying with her own partner. That worked out well since I was getting tired of this game. I decided to lead the dance myself. No one would notice if I did anyway.

He looked taken aback but I kept my innocent face on display. To anyone else it would seem like he was leading me, but we both knew I was in control. He tried to take the lead again but it was impossible since I was moving in such a way that if he purposely made a mistake we would fall, and that would make him look bad.

Sasha's expression was calm and cool, but I could tell he was feeling embarrassed and frustrated. He had wanted a challenge, so now I was giving it to him. Not that he was handling it well.

I made eye contact with Arnold. He knew what I was doing. He knew what my dance skills were like. He knew what dancing meant to me. But we both knew that I shouldn't parade it in front of Brigid's gang.

I would have told him not to worry. Because Sasha couldn't really do anything to me. And he wouldn't say a word about this incident to Brigid either. He wouldn't want other people to know he'd been controlled by a girl. It would have been too embarrassing to admit. I gave him an innocent smile.

I won. And he knew it.

Then he stepped on my foot.

I allowed him to. It was the end of the song, so I wanted him to vent a little of his frustration. I also wanted to let him know that I didn't want to be the next target. That I hoped that he wouldn't hold any grudges. That we would act like nothing had happened. I was about to act like an innocent girl who'd fallen for his charms when a loud voice echoed throughout the gym.

"Sasha, you shouldn't step on a lady's foot!"

We turned to the teacher, who was staring at us. We were both surprised. I didn't realise she'd been paying attention to us. The whole class turned to look. I had to act fast. I was going to pretend to be clueless, but then he turned towards me, looking apologetic.

"I'm so sorry."

The gym went dead silent. No one seemed to breathe.

This was going to be a problem.

Realising what she had done, the teacher said, "Alright, you may all go home now. I'll see you next week, same time and place."

Everyone moved to collect their bags. Arnold grabbed ours and I rushed towards him. But I could feel the eyes on my back.

This was becoming worse with every passing second. Sasha apologised to me? No one in Brigid's group would ever apologise. I couldn't believe it. He did that on purpose. Because of this little incident, Brigid might set her sights on a new target very soon.

Sighing internally and keeping my emotions in check, I tried to get out of the gym as quickly as I could. Arnold was right next to me, grabbing onto my arm.

Brigid is eyeing you right now! Let's get to the car quickly.

There could only be one solution right now.

Outside the gym, most of our class was still around. They were staring at me, whispering about me. Perfect. I turned to Arnold and smiled. I took a step, and at that moment, I tripped.

The gym was on top of a small hill. So when I tripped, I rolled and landed at the entrance to the science building. I was covered in sand, grass and dirt. Everyone in the class burst out laughing while I lay on the grass and checked the weather.

Dark clouds formed within a second. I tried not to think much of the pain. I focused on the sky. I focused on my emotions.

It doesn't even hurt. I have no injuries. I feel no pain. It should not hail. I am fine. I don't feel anything.

As fast as the dark clouds had formed, they

disappeared, leaving the sky crystal clear. It was as if nothing had happened. I closed my eyes. Thank the winter ancestors. At least that had worked. Thank the winters it did. I slowly sat up.

"Layla, are you okay!?"

Arnold bolted down the hill and gently dusted my back. I didn't say anything. I acted like I was embarrassed and on the verge of tears. Brigid and her gang walked past me slowly – all looking down on me.

"She totally deserved it," Brigid whispered, loudly enough for me to hear.

Her gang snickered and left. Our class had also started to move on with their own lives. When they were out of range, Arnold went into full panic mode and I dropped the act.

"Why did you have to do that to yourself? What if your injuries had been worse? What if you actually made it hail? What if–"

I put my hand on top of his and gave him a small smile.

"Even though I felt the fall, I did control my emotions. That's all that matters."

Arnold was shaking his head. "Was falling really necessary?"

I looked him right in the eye.

"I'd rather hurt myself than let them hurt me."

CHAPTER THREE

"Couldn't you have done something else? Something safer? Something that doesn't require changing the weather?" Arnold rambled on, holding onto me as we headed towards the car park.

I stopped.

"The bus is that way." I pointed in the opposite direction. He glared at me. "So what were you saying?" I looked at all the cars in the school parking lot and continued in that direction.

I knew if he had a choice he would have called an ambulance and made me rest for the entire month. He was already carrying my bag as well as his and had his arm around me, supporting my weight. I wasn't even injured, but I allowed him to, otherwise he'd have nagged at me for the entire year.

"If I hadn't done that, do you think Brigid would have got my message?" I said in answer to his question, but he looked confused.

"What message?"

"That I'm afraid of her."

He looked even more confused. "Haven't we already been doing that since we got here?"

"Not when I tried to sidestep Sasha today. Since I was brave enough to embarrass her favourite, that would mean I would be brave enough to embarrass her, right?"

"Yes..."

"We both know she'd never allow anyone to embarrass her, so she wouldn't have let me off that easily. But if I'd admitted my mistake, then she'd know I only wanted to protect myself in a moment of defence. And if I punish myself, it shows I'm still terribly afraid of her wrath."

We reached the end of the car park. I could see our old white car, which he'd parked in the corner, away from all the others. He kept quiet as he opened the door and gently let me in.

"How exactly does falling down a hill and injuring yourself show that you're afraid of her?" he asked, getting into the driver's seat. "This is exactly my point. You could have done something else."

"Right before I fell, I made eye contact with Brigid. And because I acted like I was afraid of her, I *accidently* lost my step. I fell right in front of an audience that would spread the embarrassing news about me. The whole performance would have satisfied her."

I thought back. As expected, she'd been watching me. So when I smiled at Arnold, I saw Brigid and knew that was my cue. Then she made a comment and smirked, and I knew the plan had worked.

I studied Arnold's face. Even though everything I said made sense, I knew he didn't like any of it. I didn't like it either but with the circumstances that we were in, what else could we do? We were confined to restrictions and if we broke them, we'd be back to where we started.

"Don't worry, she won't know that I was acting. I allowed her to look down on me."

Arnold was still silent as he started the engine and drove off.

"It did not hail. Nobody was hurt. I also feel well."

"Why do you always–"

"Before you continue, you have to acknowledge the fact that the performance was what saved us from becoming her next target."

"Yes, but–"

"It's more important than anything that we don't become her target, right?"

"There had to be a better way."

"But that was the easiest way to solve the problem."

He turned left at the traffic lights instead of right.

"Aren't you going to practise?" I asked.

"I decided not to today."

"You can't do that! How can you stay as my bodyguard if you aren't the best?"

"Even with my arms and legs tied up, I could beat all the guards they have trained."

"That's because you trained every single day without rest to make it this far."

I remembered the days when he didn't sleep at all so that he could control his powers. The days when we were stuck in one place. The days when no one believed such a feat could have been accomplished by an Unwintle, a term used for those who are not of age. Arnold and I, we struggle with our powers since they were not fully developed. Whereas Maria, a Wintle, is fully able to control hers, even in human form. That was why Arnold's training was so important.

"I'll stay in the car while you practise. You'll lose to Maria if you don't keep practising."

"We are going home so you clean and treat your wounds."

Wounds?

Then I looked at myself. There were red scratches on my arms and a long scrape on my leg. It wasn't too bad. It didn't even hurt. I was about to argue, but Arnold looked at me sadly. "If you don't present yourself well tonight, it won't look good."

I didn't speak. I couldn't argue with that. He was right – I had alerted them that I was hurt. I would need to convince them again tonight. So I would need to present myself well or else I would lose the battle.

"Maybe home school was the better choice," Arnold muttered.

"And have one of the Ministers keep an eye on us? Again?" He knew we couldn't afford to have that. Not unless we wanted the Ministers to discover Arnold making winter. "If you think about it, I did a decent job of injuring myself. It's not as bad as I thought it would have been."

"How badly were you going to injure yourself?"

I raised an eyebrow at him. "You know the answer. Whatever is necessary."

"No, you chose the riskiest way to solve the problem. You're always like this. Why haven't you learned your lesson from..."

I kept silent as Arnold kept talking. I knew that would distract him for a little bit. I looked out into the sky, lost in my thoughts. I would do anything that was necessary. Like how I did that day. I remembered it clearly. I sat on my throne looking down from the dais to the Ministers who stood in lines of four. They wanted to have a meeting. But I knew that it was much more.

"Your Majesty, as the youngest Queen we understand your struggle with your new powers since you don't have the previous Queen to mentor you. But your paperwork needs to be addressed as they keep piling. So we would like to suggest a solution. As you solely focus on making winter weathers, we think it's best that we appoint a Regent to handle the duties of the Queen," the Minister of Education said.

I smiled and listened politely. But inside, dread piked throughout my body. They wanted to make me a puppet Queen. They wanted to lock me in that room and create only weather. They wanted to control everything that happens in Winterland. They wanted to create war.

I cannot let that happen.

"Are you suggesting that I am incompetent?" I asked.

"We do not dare to suggest such a thing. We are merely suggesting for someone as experienced like Halwende to govern until you are able to control the new Queen's power," the Minister of People said.

I sat up straighter and stared right at the Old Man. Halwende, the Minister of Rites. The Minister who has served the very first Winter Queen and all the others that followed. The Minister who overlooked the other Ministry. The Minister who must have waited for this opportunity to gain power. I would not give it to him. So I asked, "Why can't I do both?"

Murmurs scattered across the room. Doubts were voiced.

I continued to only stare at him and said, "Why don't we try something? To prove my capability not only will I create the winter weathers and handle the duty of a Queen, but I am confident I will be able to excel in school and survive the human world."

Silence descended in the room as understanding dawned on them. Then chaos erupted.

"Your Majesty, that would be absurd."

"Your Majesty, it is too risky!"

"An outrageous idea, Your Majesty."

It was a weak proposition. One I knew no doubt would be rejected. A gamble. But I had to try. And I would die trying. Because if he became Regent, it was over for me. It was over for Winterland. The entire world will be destroyed. He was staring at me and I stared right back at him. Then he slowly said, "What has Your Majesty planned?"

I couldn't believe my ears; the Old Man was giving me a chance. I didn't give it a second thought – I took it.

I held my head high and spoke in a clear loud voice. "I will descend to Earth. There I will create winter weathers from the oceans or other water bodies. I will no longer hurt others and have access to all the water to make weather. This would create weather faster and will give me more time so I would be able to handle all the paperwork. With our first recent deaths, we do not want to invoke more fear in the public. As the leader, I will survive the human world and prove that we are safe. That humans are not a threat to us."

I looked around. The horrified looks weren't very encouraging but I spoke as if we moved forward with the plan, "I'll need a servant who can cook and clean. And since we only have one servant in Winterland who can, I will take Maria with me. Then we will hold a tournament for my bodyguard. Only the best can protect me. During the time I'm away in case something does happen, please raise an army but in secrecy. We do not want to alarm the public. Once I come of age and arrive back, we can discuss future plans." Then I held up three fingers. "Three warnings. If I do anything wrong that shows my incapability, then I will come back and we will have a Regent."

I internally prayed to our Winter ancestors. I only needed his approval. Once he approved, the rest of the Ministers wouldn't argue. Even if this didn't work out,

I would try something else. But this was the best. This was what I needed. I had to escape from that room. I had to escape the watchful eyes of the Ministers. And the only place I could was the human world, even if I hated them. Even if it was a risk.

Surely he would be able to see that it benefitted both of us. Even though he didn't get full reign, he still was able to get the one thing he wanted. An army. We waited in silence for the Old Man to raise any concerns. To object. But to my greatest surprise, he bowed.

"You are our newly appointed Queen. We will follow as you suggested." Everyone in the room froze. Then the Old Man stood up straight. "But if anything happens then I hope you understand that you would need to take full responsibility."

No one said a word. They all just stared at the Old Man. I hid my shock and stood with confidence I never knew I had. "Excellent. Then it is settled. We will get this started at once."

I descended the stairs. I did it. I got what I wanted. It was a miracle that it worked. Because it could have gone entirely wrong. But how could he have agreed without any argument? How could he allow me? Was it because I gave him what he wanted? Did he see my resolve? Or did he pity me?

As I landed on the last step, I looked into his cold

hard stare and a cold chill ran down my spine. That was the moment I knew. If he didn't become Regent. If I wasn't his puppet Queen. Then I was no longer of any use to him.

He was already planning on my death.

He must have chosen this school knowing Brigid would harm me or I would harm her. If he thought I voluntarily walked to my death in the human world, then he underestimated me. But it was because of that, I was able to escape Winterland and train Arnold in case something happened to me. Just a year left. I will survive whatever gets thrown at me. But I had to admit that today was a close one.

Thank the world that the weather didn't change. At least one thing worked in my favour. That was a risk I was willing to take. Between the two options I had, it made sense that I would choose to rely on the weather. Brigid already knew my weakness. It would be easy for her to destroy me if she had a reason to. Throughout these years I had given her no reason to target me. This could have been it. All my efforts would have been wasted. If I had not thought of falling... I didn't want to think of a new solution if I hadn't.

But now we had gotten her attention. She would keep an eye on us from now on. So that meant we would need to be more careful in the future until we were off her potential target list. And we'd been doing so well for so long. Curse Sasha...

"Promise?" He pulled up in our driveway and turned off the engine. He stared at me.

"I refuse." He kept staring at me, but I was defiant in my answer, even though I hadn't heard what the "promise" was in reference to. I had an idea anyway.

He leapt out of the car and round to my side and lifted me up in his arms. I crossed my arms instead of wrapping them around his neck because this was entirely unnecessary.

"Mum!" he yelled.

CHAPTER FOUR

"She purposely fell!"

Arnold paced the lounge room while Maria and I ate our droplet cakes. He had been repeating the same statement for the past hour. I wasn't surprised that he hadn't given up yet. When he wanted a promise from me, he would keep arguing until I gave it to him.

"And why did she do it?" Maria asked him in a bored voice.

"I get it. But that's why it's even more important that she promises never to do it again." He stopped and looked at me.

Ignoring his gaze, I took a bite from my droplet cake. I kept my face neutral. But this cake wasn't the best of Maria's creations. Tonight we had a completely opaque blue cake. It had a spicy but sour taste. Not a good combination.

I still said nothing. He started pacing again and started in with his next favourite statement. "Because at that time–"

Maria gave me a meaningful look. So I said, "How about if I promise I'll try not to do it again?"

Arnold stopped and thought for a moment. Then he nodded. "I'll take that promise."

Maria sighed and said, "Why couldn't you promise that earlier? All the walking and talking was driving me crazy, dear."

I smiled. If I wanted Arnold to stop nagging, it was always best to let him talk until he knew that he couldn't convince me otherwise. But if I met halfway, then he would too.

"You promised! You can't change it now." Arnold smiled and sat on the couch, finally starting to eat his droplet cake. Then he made a face. I tried not to laugh. Maria caught his expression and glared at him.

She turned towards me. "Poor Layla. But that was really quick thinking. Although, don't you think Sasha will do something in revenge?"

"He shouldn't stir any more trouble. But for someone who's not afraid to make a scene, I wouldn't be surprised if he tried to do something else."

"Of all the people you had to partner with, why did it have to be Brigid's second in command?" Arnold shook his head.

"Was that who he was?"

Arnold just looked at me and shook his head again. "I shouldn't have been surprised," he muttered.

That was true. I have the worst memory when it comes to people unless they were important.

He sighed, looked at me again and began his explanation. "Sasha Reynold is second in charge, subordinate to Brigid. He takes over when she's not around. You didn't know who he was and you still dared to risk it?"

"I knew he was a favourite."

Arnold just shook his head.

Even though I didn't know who exactly he was at the time, I knew I was risking becoming a target when I dodged every deliberate dance misstep that Sasha made. But I couldn't let him humiliate me and pretend that I was fine with it. I already had other people humiliating me.

Sasha Reynold... He hid his emotions and thoughts really well. Unfortunately for him, I could still read them. I could also tell that he was someone with pride and who hated to lose.

"Not only that, but he's also the most popular guy

in our school, "Arnold went on. "He makes all the girls fall for him and all the guys admire him. That's why he's the one who brings in people to become a part of Brigid's gang."

"I cannot believe those lines work on girls. It made me cringe, listening to those words."

"That must have been fun," Maria teased.

I made a face. "It was definitely not."

Arnold and Maria let out small giggles. Then Arnold turned serious. "I still can't believe the teacher singled you both out. Right in front of everyone as well."

If I had known the teacher was watching us, I wouldn't have let him step on my foot. Then again, judging by his reaction he also didn't know the teacher was watching, or else he wouldn't have made a scene. I was sure that he wouldn't want others to know he lost to a girl. He just acted faster.

If I had reacted sooner and played the innocent girl, Brigid would never have known. But maybe that was what it was. Sasha knew I didn't want him to make a scene, but he did. If he hadn't, he'd have lost to me even more than he already had. It was a reminder for me that even if he lost, he had someone who could defeat me in a second.

What a coward. Hiding behind his leader. I shouldn't be surprised. Everyone in Brigid's gang was the same.

"Right now it would be best to avoid him," I said and they nodded.

"And what if he comes at us?" Arnold asked.

"This is where I need your knowledge of everyone in the school."

Arnold smiled immediately, then frowned. "I would tell you now, but unfortunately we need to leave."

I looked at the clock. He was right. It was nine.

The silence stretched out. None of us wanted to go.

Arnold walked towards the door and I stood up. Maria handed me her paperwork. At times like this, I wished that I was a little child again. When I wasn't the Queen, when I still had my aunt and when I could do anything I wanted. I followed him out to the car.

"Be extra careful in future," Maria called out. We nodded and got in.

Arnold backed out of the driveway and set off. I looked out at the unfamiliar roads that we passed along.

"Where are we heading tonight? Have we been there?" We were driving on a deserted road.

"No, it's a first. I didn't think it safe to go back to the same beach as yesterday."

"But who would go out this late anyway?"

"Layla, are you going to be alright?"

I knew he was going to ask me that. I tried to distract him, but I failed. From his tight grip on the steering wheel, I could tell he was trying hard to concentrate on the road.

"In all honesty, I think it might be our first warning."

Arnold's eyes widened. I thanked the clear skies his hands were glued to the wheel.

"I was just joking. It didn't hail, so everything should be alright."

"Please tell me. The truth."

I didn't say anything but my silence confirmed his thoughts.

Arnold nodded. "Understood."

It was times like these that I felt the most guilty. When Arnold got blamed for all the mistakes that *I* made, even when I tried to defend him. I tried hard to control my emotions. But my powers were unstable. That was why I avoided confrontation with Brigid.

There were enemies all around me. I could only handle them one at a time. Brigid was an immediate threat, whereas I could deal with the Ministers later. Even when the Minsters were harder to deal with.

We arrived in a dark and empty car park surrounded by trees and bushes. I wasn't sure if we were near water. But when I put the window down a little, I could hear the crashing waves.

We were at a beach. It was a good location since it had a large amount of water but at the same time, it was risky. There was a higher possibility of humans being around but I trusted Arnold's choices. I waited in the car as he got out and did an area search. Just listening to the waves crashing onto the shore made me relax.

When Arnold came back, I knew it was time for me to go. I took the towel that we always kept in the car and wrapped it around my head. Then I followed him towards the beach. The cold wind was strong and every step into the sand drew us closer to the water.

Ahead was completely dark. Human eyesight was weak. But the streetlights behind us were bright enough to light our way. I wanted to say something, but at this point knew that whatever I said wouldn't make him feel any better, so I kept silent.

I waited at the edge of the water as Arnold did a quick last area search. I stared at the black waters while the wind got stronger and colder. He returned, checked on me and walked into the water. He swam as far as he could and disappeared into the water.

I looked around me; seeing no one. I transformed into my original form. My long, light blue hair cascaded in waves down my back and my skin tingled with the power I'd kept hidden. Now my human body could finally sleep.

Arnold's head appeared above the water and he transformed. My hair whipping in the wind, I walked into the water and floated over to Arnold. His blue eyes looked into my blue eyes. He was ready and nervous. I patted his head and he gave me a small smile. Then we dived deep into the ocean. We both sank to the very bottom and our feet landed on the sand.

I waved my hand in front of me. Arnold took a few steps away so that he wouldn't be seen. A few seconds later, a big clear screen appeared, connecting to Winterland. It showed the Ministers standing in the throne room, waiting for my appearance. As always, they did not seem happy.

"Your Majesty." They kneeled down to me. There were more Ministers than normal. Of course, there would be more tonight. But there was one person I couldn't see.

"You may rise. Did something happen? Why are there so many people gathered here today?" I asked innocently. Even though I couldn't see him, I know he was there. I could feel his presence over the connection.

"We should ask if you're safe, Your Majesty. What happened today? How did you get injured?" the Minister of Work asked.

"Thank you for your concern. I injured myself slightly. It is not a big problem."

"Your health is our highest concern, Your Majesty," the Minister of People stated.

I wanted to scoff. As if they truly cared about my well-being. I kept my emotions in check. I didn't want to cause Perth to have a massive thunderstorm and then have to explain why there was one in front of them.

"You have to take care better care of yourself, Your Majesty," the Minister of People continued.

"I know, I was–"

"No, it's that servant, Arnold," the Minister of Education said.

Arnold tensed.

"Ministers–"

"Your Majesty, what if he's trying to plot something against you? What if he is just like his father?" one said.

"He's a son of a traitor. A servant. He shouldn't be the one to protect you," another said.

Others added their opinions.

"We should hold another competition to choose a new bodyguard for you."

"Or it's better for Your Majesty to return."

"Yes, it's not safe for you in the human world. Please consider returning to your world."

They must have planned this, because they all bowed down and said, "Please reconsider."

They gave me no respect. They stopped me from speaking and tried to pressure me to give in to their requests. They had always been like this. Nothing had changed since the day I was crowned. I clenched my fist. I kept my emotions in check again and smiled as I looked around for signs of him. The Old Man was still silent. Of course, he would let the Ministers complain.

"Ministers, you haven't asked me how I got injured. Wouldn't you like to know the reason first?"

"He is meant to protect you from any harm. Any injury you sustain is his responsibility," the Minister of Education said.

They always made Arnold the problem. That would never change. I didn't want to look at Arnold's expression. I knew hearing all this hurt him every time.

"Even if I got a paper cut while doing paperwork?"

I showed them a small red line across my index finger. They all went silent and stood straight. I had come prepared.

Earlier, while Arnold was having his rant, I was drawing on my finger so that it looked like I had a cut. No one other than myself should handle the paperwork, so Arnold couldn't possibly have been near me when I was doing it. Although, they didn't need to know I always worked in front of them and was teaching Maria how to handle the paperwork.

My dress was long enough to cover all my other injuries so they couldn't see them. And without closer inspection, they would be unable to recognise that it was a fake injury. I knew this would stop them from blaming Arnold and as a result, would also stop them from taking me back. Because that was their ultimate goal.

The Ministers had no response as I knew they would. I wanted to smile but instead acted nonchalant and let my hand drop. They wanted to lock me up again. *I won't let that happen.*

"Please be careful, Your Majesty," the Minister of Work said.

I nodded. "I will."

"But speaking about your safety, we believe it's best if you had more Wintles to protect you."

I stared down at the Minister of People. He was always the one bold enough to speak out. He was always on the Old Man's side. "That would draw unnecessary attention. We have discussed this."

"We could hardly believe that Arnold would be the best candidate for your safety."

"He won the tournament fair and square. Who else would be better to protect me?"

"Perhaps it would be better for Your Majesty to return."

"Are you questioning my decisions?"

It was clear that they were, but the Ministers didn't say anything. I knew no one would dare to question me. Then the Old Man spoke.

"Please don't be angry. We were concerned for your

well-being. Please do reconsider."

A chill ran down my spine.

He was not concerned for me.

I was glad to be in my true form as it made it slightly easier to control my powers, otherwise I would have made the temperature around me cold. I was shocked to my inner core, even though my outer appearance seemed composed. The Minister of Rites would never say a word in our discussions or our arguments. No matter how unfavourable it was for them, he would always just silently observe. The only reason he said this was because it benefitted him.

I knew they didn't see me as their ruler, but normally they would have given up on whatever it was they wanted, after everything I had said. But I could see that wasn't going to happen tonight. This was the opportunity they had been waiting for.

It was my mistake to have injured myself. I was able to escape from their previous attacks because I had only caused small weather changes. This time was different. They all felt how hurt I was even when I tried to hide the pain. It would be harder. They wouldn't stop until they accomplished one of those goals. But between losing Arnold or gaining guards, I knew what my choice would be.

"If you insist, this would be my first warning then."

No one said a word. All the Ministers looked surprised. My face gave away nothing. This was the best choice right now. I had wanted to keep a clean record and with the recent events with Brigid, I would rather not have this warning. But if it meant we'd be able to keep the way things were, I would rather use one of them.

I continued, "I have a trial and I intend to pass it. I want to prove that there would be no more accidents after this one, I can assure you."

They were silent for a moment until they responded in unison, "Yes, Your Majesty."

"Where is my assignment for tonight?" A wave of power went through me. I summoned a list of winter weathers, made of water, to appear in my hands. Then I waved my hand and a set of paperwork made of ice flew through the screen and straight to the Ministers. "Is there anything else we need to discuss?"

"No, Your Majesty. Thank you for your hard work."

"We will meet again tomorrow, Ministers." I swept my hand across the screen, making the image of the Ministers disappear.

I closed my eyes for a moment. I would plan my next move later. The most important thing right now was to focus on making winter. As the Winter Queen, this was my main responsibility. Every night I had to make the Earth's winter weather, from the harshest blizzard to the lightest drizzle. Then the people of Winterland would distribute the weather to the allocated locations. We all worked together as one to provide the weather, even if we had our differences.

I looked at the list of winter weathers we had to make. We had to strictly follow this. Nothing more, nothing less. That was why the Ministers were never happy with me when I couldn't control my emotions.

The list was getting longer and harder. But that was fine. After what had just happened, I was more motivated. I tore off just over half the list and handed that to Arnold. I took a few steps away from him and started swirling my arms, creating a big circle full of water droplets.

I built momentum and made the droplets turn into a big underwater ice mountain. Then I started to freeze it. In a second it turned into a giant block of ice sitting on the seabed. Its tip just touching the surface of the ocean. Arnold was still creating his mountain of ice. I began to release my powers, chiselling the ice while swimming around the mountain.

It was like a recipe. By chiselling the right amount of ice at the right intensity of my power, I would create the desired winter weather. If I was asking for stormy weather, the amount and intensity would increase, while thunder would demand less ice but more of my power. The ice I chiselled would turn into tiny crystal shards that would melt into the part of the list that required the weather. Then that section would disappear and be delivered to Winterland.

I thought back to the days when I had to create the winter weathers out of thin air – out of nothing. With my powers, it was impossible. It took hours, even days just to create a country's weather for *one* day. And I had the entire world's winter weather to make. So I was locked in a room with four walls and four Wintles. They filled the room with an endless supply of water while they watched me struggle to make Winter. It was such a bleak and dark time. But now I could handle this. I looked to my side. And I had people who supported me.

So we worked through the list. And with the amount of water we had available, we wouldn't run out of materials to create winter. It was a good system we'd made. But despite it being helpful, it didn't change how difficult it was.

Without any warning, my powers lessened. It was like turning a tap on, expecting a rush of water to come out but instead only drops of water appeared. I stopped chiselling for a second and concentrated as hard as I could to increase my powers. But that didn't work. I was prepared to repeat the amount of chiselling until

I could create stormy weather. I shot my powers at the ice – and *boom!*

The explosion flung me onto the seabed; chunks of ice were propelled through the water around me. I blinked a couple of times as I lay on the floor. I slowly sat up. Arnold looked concerned, but he continued on. This wasn't the first time this had happened. We could only control so much until it started to have a mind of its own. No one would ever understand what we had to go through each night.

Then suddenly Arnold was flung onto the ground.

He still had a long way to go. But he had to work with such a small amount of my powers, so it was really hard on him. But at least he was getting better – just slowly.

The first morning light shone through the waters. We were nearly finished. My arm was aching, my mind had turned blank and my body was moving on its own. Even my ice mountain was starting to look distorted. I was about to hit my limit.

Arnold was moving slower and swayed a little. He was ready to give up. He had always been better physically than mentally. Seeing Arnold like that made me more determined. I thought back to the memory that motivated me the most. The only Minister who cared for me.

"You already have trouble with controlling your powers since you're still underage. You have absolutely no control of your powers in human form!" the Minister of Work had yelled. We were alone in my room. I had just told him my plans. "Do you understand the position you'll be in if you go? By going to the human world and being in human form, do you know that your negative emotions will dictate the weather? Just the smallest amount of emotion could lead to a weather disaster! It's completely unpredictable! And if you injure a human? You'll lose your life! Then there's the fact that you can't touch anything liquid. If you touch liquid, it will turn into ice. And if a human sees that? And then finds out your identity? They will control you! Can you handle all of that?"

I knew. I knew all of that, but I didn't care. I didn't care how hard it would be. This was nothing. If death was the solution, then I wasn't afraid. With every last bit of strength I had, I would set everything right.

With my remaining energy, I threw a burst of my powers on the ice, making the last of the winter weathers. I dropped my arms and tried to catch my breath. We were finally finished for the day. As our ice mountain turned into bubbles and the last of the list disappeared, we both fainted onto the sea floor.

CHAPTER FIVE

It was nearly the end of July. That meant the weather would turn warmer. If there were any small weather changes, it would be easier for the Ministers to notice. I could no longer use winter as my excuse. I'd have to be extra careful. What a start to the third semester. Not only did I have my first warning; but for the first time Brigid had noticed my existence.

I arrived at school and some of the other students were whispering about me and Sasha, but they were also talking about how I fell. I didn't even put any dressings on my injury, just to show everyone that I was punished yesterday. And it worked beautifully. Brigid and her group didn't touch me. And they didn't mark me as their next victim. Everything went as I had expected.

The week passed without anything eventful happening. Our second dance lesson came around and we were all in the gym again. This was where I'd have to keep my eye out for Brigid and her gang. I knew they would be waiting for a chance to strike if I made any mistake because this place would remind them of last week's event.

The teachers had divided our class, with the girls on one side of the gym and the guys on the other. The male teacher taught the boys their dance steps and the female teacher instructed the girls. Once again, Brigid and her girls were making fun of the steps, but I could sense they were watching me as well. Finally, the teachers finished teaching the cha cha and gathered everyone around.

"Alright, I think we are ready to practise with partners. Boys, choose your partners," the male teacher called out.

As Arnold walked towards me, out of nowhere Sasha appeared right next to me.

"May I have this dance?"

I stared at him. Then I stared at his hand.

I had expected this but hoped it wouldn't happen. Someone to test me. Of course, it would be him. I gave Arnold a reassuring look. Then I gave Sasha my hand as an answer. He took it and led me away from the other couples to our own space. We stood hand in hand, waiting for the music to start. I put on my act as the innocent and shy girl again. I looked everywhere but at him.

I knew he was trying to get his revenge on me. But he hadn't involved Brigid herself yet, so that meant that she didn't know anything. But it also showed he didn't want her to know at all.

"Hello, how are you?" he asked.

"Fine."

"I didn't ask how you looked."

I thought back to my conversation with Arnold when he told me more about Sasha.

"He's the charmer in the group."

"What do you mean?"

"He can capture any girl's heart if he wants to."

That's what Sasha wanted to believe. What arrogance. He must have felt embarrassed when I wasn't charmed by him. I must have been his biggest challenge. Did he really want to try again?

"What do you want?" I asked him.

He raised an eyebrow at me. I looked at him innocently while he stared back. No one was near enough to hear what I said. There was no point in pretending in front of him when he knew that I was acting. Especially when I'd dodged his feet last time. But I had to keep the appearance up since others were watching.

"Music, start!" the teacher called out.

Sasha led the dance. I thought he would try to step on my foot again, but his steps were all correct and he swayed me to the beat. I knew he was able to dance. He'd pretended to be bad at the last lesson so that he could charm all those girls.

"You still play the innocent girl, even when you speak to me like that."

I still blushed. "I know that Brigid is watching me."

Brigid had glanced at us a couple of times. Of course, she would be curious. Why would Sasha choose me as his dance partner?

Sasha nodded.

"Are you that afraid of her?"

What did he think?

He continued, "You must be curious why I chose you as my dance partner."

"Of course to test me. And also for revenge."

"Smart girl."

"So what do you want?"

"Straightforward too. I like that."

He spun me out then pulled me into his arm and we swayed.

"I want you to confess that you have feelings for me," he whispered into my ear.

Was he being serious?

"In public?" I asked.

"And you have to cling onto me even when I reject you." Then he pulled me back to face him. "Like a girl who is desperate and hopelessly in love."

"And if I refuse I'll become Brigid's target?"

"If you beg me, then I won't involve her."

We went silent as we danced to the song. I was and was not expecting that. I had thought he planned to step on my foot throughout the dance. Or maybe try to make me fall for him. But this was completely different.

"You wouldn't want anyone to know what happened between us," I stated.

"You're right, I don't. But I'm sure she'll be interested. A girl who is afraid of water. She would have fun with that."

Of course he would use that against me. Everyone knew. It was my excuse not to be near water so that my identity wouldn't be revealed. For him to threaten me with it so easily was the main reason I was afraid of Brigid. Otherwise, I wouldn't have bothered to put an act in front of them.

"But Brigid is allergic to water. She won't be able to join the fun," I said.

And that was the truth too. She wouldn't want to be near it. She was the main reason there were certain rules in place. Thanks to her it was easier for me to avoid humans. But it also showcased her power and gave her authority to abuse it.

"She can watch the show since she won't be participating."

So this was his way of getting revenge. He wanted to get back at me either through his method, which would embarrass me publicly, or through Brigid, which would hurt me physically. Either way would make me admit defeat to him. He definitely belonged to Brigid's group. They were meant for each other.

Since Brigid wasn't aware, I still had a chance to turn everything around. I could still use his secret against him so that I could get rid of his interest in me once and for all.

"That reminds me of something."

"A good something?" His eyes lit up.

"Of a boy giving a helping hand to a girl by giving away a packet of tissues." I knew that did it. I nearly missed the shock that crossed his face. But I gave him credit for hiding it so quickly. "You're really soft-hearted, aren't you?"

"Softened it up for you." His face came closer to mine.

I didn't move. His warm brown eyes bored into mine in an attempt to charm me. But I wasn't going to back down.

"I'm sure it's the same for everyone."

"Especially for you."

"Especially the victims."

His smile grew wider. A smile I was sure all girls would have fallen for. It was a shame that I was immune. If anything, it gave me confidence for what I was going to say next. He swung me out and embraced me once again and we swayed. Then I said under my breath, "You once were a victim."

His arms stiffened around me. He swung me out and pulled me back in. But this time his smile was tight. I could feel Brigid's eyes on me. She must have known something was wrong.

"What do you know about me?"

Arnold had told me he'd seen Sasha giving the latest victim a packet of tissues. With no one else around. It might not mean anything to anyone but for Sasha... If Brigid ever found her second in command comforting her target... I just smiled at him.

Not only that but a bully victim. The reputation he had worked to build would vanish right away. Truthfully, I didn't know if he had been a victim. But that was the most logical reason why he would have helped despite risking getting into trouble himself. Seeing his reaction, I must have been right. Let his imagination wander. He could think that I did a background search on him, for all I cared. I was absolutely sure that he wouldn't seek me out after this.

"If you don't say a word to Brigid, then I won't either," I answered.

He was smiling, even though I knew for a fact he was angry. He had to choose between getting his revenge or losing his position. If he chose to get his revenge, then we'd both suffer. But if he chose his position, we'd both win. It was an easy choice. The music stopped and he let me go of my hands. Then he walked away without a reply. But that was an answer that I'd gladly accept.

Arnold walked up to me as my new dance partner.

"What happened?"

"Good news," I told him.

CHAPTER SIX

Every night the Ministers would try to convince me to come back to Winterland. Every day I worked on the paperwork. At school, Brigid and her group ignored me as if nothing had happened. She had found a new victim to bully. Everything was back to how it had been before.

But when we had chemistry, the last class at the end of the week, Brigid stared right at me as she walked into the classroom. I wanted to stare right back, but instead I studied my open book and pretended to look nervous. I glanced up at Arnold. His expression was grim. He'd noticed it too. What made her look at me? Did Sasha tell her in the end?

Then Sasha walked in and went right past me

without a glance.

So maybe he hadn't said a word. But I was sure there was more to it. Did she find it odd that Sasha chose me as one of his dance partners? Or was this a show of power? Whatever the reason, I could only prepare myself in case anything were to happen. This wasn't going to be a peaceful lesson.

"When I call out your name, come up and get your test," the teacher said in a bored voice. He sounded annoyed as well but started to call names.

Arnold's shoulder touched mine. *I have a bad feeling about this.*

You have a bad feeling about everything, I answered.

But I also couldn't help but suspect the teacher. If Brigid wanted to do something, she would tamper with the order of those test papers. This would be the perfect time and opportunity to publicly humiliate me.

She could get the teacher to give you garbage duty and then use that opportunity to do something worse. Or she could trip you over. Or push you over. Even slap you. Or maybe she would–

Arnold, please calm down.

"Brigid."

Suddenly, the room's atmosphere felt heavier.

Arnold gripped his hands together tightly. The girl who was called before hurried to her seat. Brigid smiled as she walked up to the front of the classroom to get her test paper. She must have enjoyed everyone's reaction.

I found it all ridiculous. If everyone didn't fear her, she wouldn't have the power to control everyone in the first place. And I wouldn't need to pretend to fear her right now, just to conceal my identity.

Suddenly a blast of wind passed through the window. The books on the tables fluttered wildly, the cupboards rattled and even the skeleton at the front danced on its stand. Everyone in the room was either shocked or laughing.

Arnold didn't react, but I could tell he was surprised. Even I was a little surprised by my powers. I took a deep breath. *Layla, keep your emotions in check – you can't feel annoyed.*

Arnold patted my hand. He knew what I felt. That I couldn't help it. He knew I was trying to control my emotions and that it was hard.

I patted his hand as well. I had to do better. There was more at stake if I made a wrong move. And everything would be fine after we got over this hurdle.

"Someone close that window!" the teacher yelled out. "Layla."

That would not be a coincidence. Arnold made to get up, but I stopped him. I had to be the one to get it. Because that is what Brigid would want.

I got out of my seat and tried to act scared, like everyone else. Brigid was definitely going to do something. Arnold was right when he listed all the things that she could do. But I didn't think she would do anything physical. After all, I wasn't her marked victim. I was a few metres away from Brigid. She turned around and dropped her test paper right in front of me.

"Oh, oops. Is it okay if you pick that up for me? My back is really hurting," she said with her hands behind her back, massaging, smiling innocently at me.

I looked at her and then at the paper. Bracing myself for the worst, my senses alert, I bent down. Maybe she was going to get violent after all. It would have been the perfect opportunity to hurt me. A warning. As I reached for the paper, she moved fast… and stepped on the edge.

I looked up at her, expecting a slap across the face, but she didn't do anything. That was when I realised – she wanted me to bow down to her. Brigid was looking down at me, smirking, her hands behind her back. Standing as if she ruled the world. Looking at me as if I was beneath her and was nothing but an object of her amusement.

There was a glint in her eyes. She wanted to let everyone know who was in control. A reminder of what she was capable of. The class was silent, watching. Time felt like it slowed down to this moment. Everyone waited for what Brigid would do next. They waited for my response. My grip on the paper tightened.

I bow down to no one. I am Queen of Winters. I control the winter weathers.

I could have frozen her to death and melted her to a drop with a single thought if I'd wanted to. How dare a self-centred lowly human mock me! I looked down and closed my eyes and took deep, quiet breaths.

Don't let it get to you.

Don't feel anything.

Don't let them win.

It's not worth it.

I tugged the paper from beneath her foot, stood up and looked nervously at her.

"Here you go." I held it out to her with my two shaking hands.

She was pleased. It was my pride. I was willing to give my pride away if I was going against Brigid. If I had acted any differently, it could have been a lot worse. For the bigger picture, I could lower myself this time.

"Thank you so much." She said it so cheerfully I knew I no longer held her attention.

I stepped aside. She smiled at me again and started walking. I kept it together. I looked over at Arnold. He looked like he was going to cry. He must have been so proud of me. I was relieved too. I did it. I endured it. We made it through. We were safe.

Brigid carried on toward her seat and was just about to pass the skeleton stand. If only that skeleton would fall on top of her. It would make me feel a lot better. She didn't deserve to be treated as someone so important. She should feel what she made the rest of us felt – humiliation. As if I could suddenly completely control my powers, the skeleton stand started to fall over.

This could not be happening.

I dashed and reached out a hand for it.

I missed.

The skeleton fell right on top of Brigid and brought her down to the floor. To her credit, she caught it in time so that it wouldn't crush her – but then she also kissed it.

"Ewww!" Her scream was so loud that I was sure the whole corridor could hear her.

She pushed it away from her and touched her lips. I caught it and pushed it back to standing. If the class was silent before, this was a deadly silence. You couldn't hear a breath. The only sound was the air-conditioning, making the room as cold as I felt.

I didn't dare to breathe. I couldn't feel anything. If she was injured, I was going to die. I was not allowed to injure a single human. A human should not sustain any bleeding injury. This was my end. I searched my inner core to see if it had disappeared. If it was smashed.

I waited for another heartbeat. Another second passed. Nothing happened. I slowly exhaled. She was okay. There was no blood injury. My inner core was still intact. I was still alive. I sighed internally. Thanked the winter ancestors.

"Stop messing with Mr Skeleton and get back to your seat," the teacher barked and started calling names again as if nothing had happened.

The class started whispering and snickering. That was when I came back to reality. I slowly looked at Brigid. Who gave me a look that would devour me. I stared at her. Things had just taken a turn for the worst. Just when everything was finally getting back to normal.

CHAPTER SEVEN

"How could this be happening?" Arnold paced back and forth.

We were in the lounge room and had just told everything to Maria. I poked at my droplet cake. Tonight it was the flavour of thunder so it was popping in my mouth. But I was too preoccupied to appreciate it.

"But I have to say Layla, you controlled that wind well!" Maria was smiling at me, trying to be positive. I returned it weakly.

"That was most likely the last time that she will be able to do it," Arnold pointed out.

He was right. It was just luck that I controlled my powers at the worst possible time. I created that wind.

That rarely happens. It should never have happened. But it did. And now I was suffering over something I should have been proud of. At least it was a gentle one, no one had noticed. But strong enough to topple a skeleton.

Brigid must have thought I pushed the skeleton over since I was an arm's length away from it. And on top of that, the teacher yelled at her. In front of the class. She wouldn't be able to stand the humiliation. She would never forgive me for that.

I still couldn't believe everything that had happened. I'd been so careful for so long. I'd avoided her, acted the weakling and even intentionally hurt myself. And because of one hurt, ego-inflated teenage boy, who started it all, everything had gone out of my control.

I put the plate aside and leaned my head back onto the armchair. Maybe I should've let Sasha step on my foot multiple times. Pretend that I was charmed by him. Lie that he was the most handsome man that ever lived on this planet. Maybe then he wouldn't have given me his attention. Then, in turn, maybe Brigid wouldn't have given me attention. So that I wouldn't have to deal with this right now.

"What are we going to do?" Arnold whispered.

Maria and Arnold were looking at me. No. If I were to go back to that time, I would do it all over again. I was already careful with Brigid. And then there were the Ministers, who looked down on me. I would never forgive myself if I became an object of Sasha's amusement as well. Especially when the dance lessons were supposed to make me forget about everything.

No one would ever humiliate me unless I allowed them to. This was just a minor setback that no one expected. That was all there was to it. Something that we could fix. We could get back to our normal lives soon. I grabbed the plate and took a bite of my cake.

"We can't avoid her."

"Yes," Arnold said. "Do you remember that time when there was a girl who was caught hiding in the girls' toilet every day and then they–"

"We can only wait for three days and then pay up," I said and took another bite.

"That simple?"

"Very simple."

There were only two ways to save yourself from Brigid's wrath. One was to wait for that wrath to pass by and suffer the abuse. The other was to pay upfront so that she could throw a party to cheer herself up.

"Would it be that easy?" Arnold looked worried.

"I've always thought of this, just in case we were ever her target. And it is very simple. She made that rule thinking no one would ever be able to pay her. She wanted to show people how rich she was. Fortunately for us, we have the funds ready. And we have the weekend to pretend that we're having a hard time. We could avoid getting hurt and also stop becoming the target."

I paused for a moment then continued, "If there was any problem, then it would be that Brigid would be disappointed that she didn't get a chance to unleash her wrath. The only way we can escape from that is by fulfilling whatever demand she makes."

Arnold opened his mouth to speak. I held a hand up. "I know. Before you say anything, I know. But it's better than continuing to be her target. One day isn't going to hurt us. I'll endure whatever she wants me to do if it means our freedom."

Arnold did not like the idea at all. I could tell he was trying to think of a different plan, but he nodded. He knew it was the only thing we could do. Then I looked at Maria. "I'm sorry we have to bother you this time."

Maria smiled at me brightly. "Sweetie, that money is sitting there doing nothing. It's not a bother at all! As long as you're safe that is all that matters." She stood and came over to hug me.

Arnold started to relax, but then I said,

"You're going to school on Monday without me."

That made him jump out of his chair.

"Why?!"

"Because she'll know that I know I'm the target since you'll see the mark on my locker."

"Why wait for Tuesday? Why can't we just pay her Monday? We don't have time to wait." Arnold started pacing again.

"We can't be a step ahead of her or else she'll be even more upset with me than she already is. We have to pretend that we struggled with the news. Since she hasn't marked me yet, she won't show up this weekend. We'll be safe for now."

"You can't stay home by yourself! Did you forget when a guy stayed home for a week and Brigid's gang broke into his house, dragged him back to school and–"

I wanted to emphasise that I was only going to stay at home for *one* day but Maria sat back and interrupted him. "He has a point, Layla. Do you want me to stay home with you?"

I looked at both of them. They were the loveliest people and I didn't deserve them.

"Don't worry. If Brigid asks, tell her that I felt sick because I was scared. To be safe, on Monday when we go down for our meeting, I'll stay in the water for the entire day until you get there."

"During the day? Where people can see you?" Arnold remarked, but he was starting to seem a lot calmer.

"During the day, when no one else will be around."

Arnold did not look convinced, but he didn't argue any further. He knew that being in the water was safer than anywhere else here on Earth. I walked towards Arnold and patted him on the head. He let me.

"Even if a human finds me, they would need to know my full name and true identity. How are they going to know that? I'll be in my true form so if they do see a glimpse of me, they'll probably think I'm one of those made-up mermaid creatures. It'll be fine."

He nodded.

"Come on. Let's go meet the Ministers."

CHAPTER EIGHT

The sun shone through the depths of the ocean. I slowly opened my eyes and sat up. I looked at Arnold, who was already standing.

"Your Majesty, I need to leave now."

I stood up too. "You're calling me Your Majesty again. You know better than to listen to them."

A silence fell between us. During the weekend, Arnold was able to practise while Maria and I focused on the paperwork. Our weekend routine didn't change. Nothing happened, as I predicted. Today I would be officially marked as Brigid's victim. Arnold didn't look happy to leave at all.

"Alright, go to school and act like you're scared.

I'll be here."

He frowned even more. "Are you sure–"

"If you don't hurry, you're going to miss school."

He looked like he was going to throw a tantrum but then thought better of it. He lingered for another moment and then jetted away.

I sighed. He would never stop worrying about me. But without him, it was very quiet. I looked around. It was just murky salt water. But the water had different patterns to its usual movements. I guessed that some early swimmers were entering the water.

I floated further out into the ocean. Feeling cheeky, I twirled. It felt great to be in my natural form. Nothing restricting my powers. Not that I could control it entirely, but I was more comfortable. I felt the waters. It was only morning. I had an entire day to myself. Where should I go?

That's when I thought of Ningaloo Reef. Arnold had always talked about destinations we should visit if we had time to travel. I told him we'd never have time to travel overseas. So he mentioned nearby places instead. Even though I'd told him we didn't have time for road trips either, I had been listening. I couldn't help but be curious. I also wanted to go see what a reef looked like.

Since it wasn't a holiday season, not a lot of people would be there. Perfect. I surged towards the north.

I increased my sense of range in case any ships were nearby. But that didn't slow me down. It was great to be travelling in the water. And I was going so fast! I spun a few times just because I was so happy. I was so tempted to jump out of the water and leap across the surface, like a dolphin flying over the ocean. But I knew better.

I was getting close. More sea animals were swimming past. So I started to slow down and floated towards the reef. I swam closer to a group of rocks. And when I looked behind it, I was stunned. Ningaloo Reef was beautiful. There were endless coloured corals of green, blue, and red in so many different shapes and sizes. And even more schools of fish clustered together at different corals.

I checked the water movements for any signs of humans nearby. When I was sure there weren't any, I moved closer to the middle, where I was surrounded by corals and fishes. I tried to touch a black-striped yellow fish, but it quickly dodged. I giggled. It was adorable. I spent the next couple of hours swimming with the fish. Some of them joined me, while others swam away and that made me chase them. At one point, I was racing with a turtle. But of course, I always won.

It was midday and I was observing a reddish-pink coral when something tapped me on my shoulder. That turtle must have wanted another race. I spun around and was faced with Arnold instead. I stared at him. He smiled at me.

I hadn't even sensed him, even though I was alert at all times. Had it been Maria, I would have sensed her presence right away. As Unwintles, Arnold and I were unable to sense each other. We could sense a Wintle, but they were unable to sense us. That was an advantage and disadvantage.

I should have still been able to detect water movement. But the way Arnold was smiling, he must have been swimming like the fish so I wouldn't be able to. I shook my head and sighed. I sat on the seabed. Arnold sat next to me.

"Answer all my unasked questions," I said.

"I didn't like the entire plan. At all. You would be by yourself in the ocean where *anything* could happen. You could get eaten by a shark, or get lost, or get caught in a net or worse, be *seen*. You can't be by yourself without anyone to protect you. I knew I had to come back. But how? So I went to school and saw the mark on your locker. I didn't even need to act scared because I was. And for so many different reasons too. Then I realised, what if I was so scared that I couldn't stand being at school any longer and cried for home? That's what Brigid would think if she saw me like that, right? And so that's what I did. But don't worry, I passed on the message that you were sick when one of Brigid's gang tried to stop me and asked about you. I ran to the car and went back to the beach where you *should* have been. But then you weren't there. I panicked. So I searched for you everywhere, but then I remembered you seemed interested when I mentioned about a reef. And so here I am. Wasn't I smart?"

He smiled so proudly. Of course Arnold would come for me. I couldn't help but smile back as I shook my head. I couldn't get angry at him. At least Brigid now believed that I fell sick because I was scared. And she knew that I knew I was her newest target. Everything was still within my plans.

"We should head back now." I stood up.

Arnold pouted. "We never get an opportunity to have a break. Why don't we take a small one right now?"

"No, Arnold. Now that you're here, you can focus on your training and I can do my paperwork. We should take this opportunity to get better."

"Of course, but we're out here at Ningaloo Reef where it's safe." I raised an eyebrow at that. "I made sure that it was safe for us. Why not take a very short break?"

It was very rare for us to have time to relax. I guess we did have the whole afternoon off. And since he'd just arrived, a little time here wouldn't hurt. "Only for an hour."

Arnold nodded and smiled so brightly it was like looking at the sun. I started giving him a tour, but he ended up showing me around, telling me what each and every thing was. He must have always wanted to be here if he studied all these corals and fishes. We started to play around with the fish and the turtle I had raced. I kept winning, but I suspected Arnold went easy on me.

When the hour had passed, we agreed that it was time to work. We debated whether to stay under the water or to go to the surface. In the end, we decided it was best for us to be on top since he'd need more practise with the air elements around him.

So we swam further west until there was no land or reef. Just the water and the seabed. Then he swam around the area to make sure there were no ships or any other humans nearby. When he came back, he nodded and we leapt out of the water.

Now I knew how it felt to be a dolphin. It was like I was flying for a second. As our feet touched the water, I made the surface around us still and smooth. I glided on top of the water, creating ripples, and did a twirl mid-air, as if I was back at home, skating on ice. I hadn't done this in ages. I'd forgotten how much fun it was. It was like being a child again.

"Layla, slow down! Or else you'll get hurt!"

I looked back and smiled but then I fell on my bottom. My

aunt gasped and rushed to me but I just laughed.

"That was so much fun! I'm going to do it again but faster!"

I stood up and skated again while my aunt shook her head and looked at me with parental love.

I stopped moving. I didn't want to think about the past so I did my paperwork on the side while watching Arnold train on the surface. He manoeuvred the waters to his command, making them and blasting to the left and then to the right. Arnold struggled when he tried to make winter weathers, but when it came to combat, he was the best. Even when his powers were unstable.

At times he would blast to the left and it would cause him to start turning to the right, but then somehow he would take control and bring it to the left. Seeing him like this, I believed he would be able to master making winter soon. As the sun began to set, we lay right next to each other, floating on top of the calm water.

"I haven't seen you skate for so long."

We stared at the clear orange-yellow sky. That was true. I really did miss being in my real form. Being myself. Not a Queen but an ordinary Layla.

"Isn't it better if we find a human who we can trust?"

I stood up and stepped on the water. Arnold did the same.

"No humans. We're not having this discussion again," I said as I stared at the setting sun.

"But if we find–"

"No."

I turned my head and glared at him. He flinched.

"But your Aunt would be heartbroken."

A gentle drizzle sprinkled on top of the surface – it made tiny ripples all around us. I turned my back towards Arnold.

"Let's go home. Maria is waiting." He didn't reply as we sunk to the bottom of the ocean.

CHAPTER NINE

When I stepped onto the school grounds on Tuesday morning, everyone stared at me as if I were walking to my execution. And I might as well have been because Brigid was leaning against my locker – waiting like the sweet lion she was. I looked down and shuffled towards her. This would be the last of Brigid. Arnold was keeping an eye on everyone. We already had to worry about Brigid. We also had to worry if any water substance would touch me.

"Hello there, Layla. I thought you ran away, what with you missing yesterday," she said in her singsong sweet voice. Her gang snickered by her side.

"I'm... I'm so sorry..." There was a crowd forming

around us already. The bigger the better, as far as Brigid was concerned.

"I heard that you were sick. God, you do look awfully pale. Are you okay?" She crossed her arms behind her back and peered into my face. Maria had helped me put on makeup so that I would look sickly. "Well, I'm glad to see you well enough to be here." She dropped her arms and her tone became angry.

"Because I was sick of waiting."

She raised her hand to strike my face.

I thrust a thick envelope at her.

"I-I was so scared throughout the entire weekend… T-that's why I fell sick… A-and then I-I found out that I was marked yesterday… A-and… S-so I got the money ready. As fast as I could." I presented it to her, both hands shaking, bowing my head.

I can do this. I can do this. She'd happily accept this and would leave me alone. Then everything would end.

No one said a word for a while.

She was not satisfied. Of course she would not be happy with just this. As if to prove my point, she changed her voice back to the sweet tone that we all knew was fake. "Wow, how could you be so fast? You didn't waste any time at all."

I clenched my teeth. I would have to do more. At least, I had expected this. I wanted to scream, but in my heart, I knew it was the only way. I swallowed my pride, closed my eyes and slowly kneeled down. Our audience gasped. Then with my head down and arms up, I offered the envelope. Brigid's gang snickered.

I still couldn't believe that I was marked. After so many years of being cautious, and now I was begging.

I am the Queen of Winters and I am on my knees.

Don't let it get to you. Don't feel anything. Don't let them win. It's not worth it.

I can do this. I can cast my pride aside for now. I can stand this humiliation.

I couldn't change the past. I could only focus on the future. Brigid probably thought she had won, but I'd led her to think that way. Brigid didn't force me. I chose this. I was the one who allowed this humiliation to happen.

Arnold clenched his hands into fists. But he knew he couldn't do anything either. He looked away. We were both at the mercy of Brigid right now.

"Why! You didn't need to kneel! Please stand up!" Brigid's tone said otherwise.

"Please accept my gift." I held it above my head towards her.

Brigid enjoyed what she was seeing. And she was taking her time savouring her victory. But she wanted more. Wanted to hurt me further. But she couldn't and she knew that. That was her rule. Her words were *her* pride. Since I had paid my way out, she couldn't touch me ever again. No matter how much she wanted to. She stepped slowly towards me and took the envelope.

It was over. She finally took it. Nothing violent happened. No weather conditions changed. We were safe. Even Arnold relaxed beside me. No more future concerns. I could finally return to focusing my energy on the Ministers instead of Brigid.

I lowered my arms and lifted my head, ready to play the overly grateful girl. But Brigid tossed the envelope towards the bin.

Everyone froze. I stared at the envelope, which had missed the bin by a few centimetres and lay on the floor right next to it. Without missing a beat, I began to tremble as if I was afraid. But inside I was thinking everything through.

What does she want?

"Oops, sorry. My bad." Brigid showed a fake smile.

"Did I-I do something wrong?"

"I wanted to see if anyone would grab the money."

I knew what she was trying to do. I closed my eyes as if humiliated, but in reality I was trying to control my emotions.

Don't let it get to you. Don't feel anything. Don't let them win. It's not worth it.

I opened my eyes. On my hands and knees, I crawled

quickly over to the envelope. With each crawl, I could hear more snickering. With each breath, I could hear the whispering. I picked it up and put it in my mouth as if I was an obedient dog. It didn't matter. I had to do this. It was the only way. Then I crawled back to Brigid, took it out and held it above my head again.

"H-here it is."

She smirked. "Why, you didn't have to pick it up like that! You could have just walked over to grab it."

"I-I wouldn't dare."

Brigid lifted her hand with the envelope in it. As if they could read her mind, one of the people in her group came behind her and took the envelope. I sneaked a peek at who it was. I had never seen him before.

"Let's see what we have here." The boy opened the envelope and took a look inside. He whistled and closed the envelope. "Quite a lot here. Anyone want it?"

He smiled and threw it to the group. As if on cue, they started to throw it around to each other. They knew the bag would rip apart. They were doing it on purpose. They wanted me to play catch. To panic.

And so I did. I started to run after the money bag, looking like I was going to cry. Begging for them to stop. But they just kept throwing it around. Some elbowed and jabbed me while others touched my body. I ignored them and focused on the envelope.

I can do this. Even if they are laughing at me. Even if they keep throwing it and the bag looks like it will fall apart soon. Even if they're taking advantage of the situation. This show won't last any longer. We are near the end. Just a little more.

They stopped throwing the envelope. All eyes were on Brigid.

So I turned around. She was holding up a hand, smirking at me. Everyone was silent, waiting for what would come next. She put her hand down and crossed her arms in front of her chest. "For someone who is so afraid of me, why are you not crying?"

I took a quick glance at our audience. They looked either shocked or scared. As if they were watching a horror movie. Then I looked at Arnold. He'd always been bad at hiding his feelings. And right now he looked like he was going to cry. Now I knew what she had wanted all along. I looked back at Brigid, who was watching me.

"Everyone knows that you want nothing to do with anyone at school. Someone who ignores everyone. Someone who doesn't show any emotions. For you to be scared of me is a given. But I would have expected more reaction from you if you are *so* frightened. Like everyone else has." Brigid was walking back and forth in front of me, her eyes never leaving mine. "You have two choices right now. One, cry and beg me to take the money. Two, take the money and you'll stay as my marked victim. And yes, when I say cry, I want tears. I want sobbing. I want sniffling. Begging for mercy. As you should."

Her eyes shone with the idea. Since she felt insulted, she was now using me as her entertainment. Knowing full well that I didn't want to be. She was determined to have it her way. There was no way out of this. She knew the truth. She knew that I wasn't afraid of her. The moment I didn't cry when she was going to slap me, she knew.

I had acted very well as someone who shivered in fear. But there was no way I could have taken the extra step and cried. That would have been worse than being Brigid's victim. The Ministers would never let that issue go.

But there were so many risks involved in being her marked victim. Mainly, revealing my secret. They would no doubt use my weakness to their advantage. And with the unpredictable control of my powers, I could injure someone. And that would destroy everything.

So she decided to play a game with me by giving me only two options. Cry tears and accept defeat or experience the tortures she had planned for me. Either one was as bad as the other. But I knew my priorities. I always had.

"If I paid you double, would you let me go?"

Everyone in the room gasped. For me to suggest such

a thing, I was looking to stay as her marked victim for the rest of my high school years. But I didn't want to cry. I could not cry. I didn't want to alert the Ministers. After all the hard work we'd put in through all these years, I didn't want to divert from the plan. I'd had enough of acting the powerless girl. I'd rather risk being her target and survive through it than ruin all the hard work.

We could endure anything.

Brigid smirked. "I have changed my mind. From this moment, I will no longer accept any kind of payment. I will stop you as the marked one as I see fit." Brigid smiled at me. "See you around, Layla."

She flipped her hair and walked away. Each member of her gang smirked at me and followed her. The envelope was on the floor next to me. I somehow locked eyes with Sasha, who was at the back of the crowd. As soon as our eyes met, he looked away and followed the group. Was that... sadness that I caught?

Slowly, the crowd dispersed as everyone whispered to each other. The news would reach every corner of the school. I closed my eyes and tried to calm myself down.

Don't let it get to you. Don't feel anything. Don't let them win. It's not worth it.

But how I wished I could rip that smile off her face.

Arnold, who had not moved or said a single word throughout the entire exchange, finally said, "Layla, it can't be…"

"The worst-case scenario."

* * *

The whole day at school, Arnold was on high alert, looking around like a madman for any sign of danger. He didn't speak a word to me. There were no words to comfort him since whatever I said would make the reality of the situation worse for him. So we were silent throughout the day, lost in our own thoughts. But oddly, after that incident, we didn't see her for the rest of the day. And I could see that made Arnold increasingly nervous with each passing hour.

When our last was finally near its end, we left early as usual. Arnold was clearly in a hurry to leave so I wordlessly followed him. Normally we would have gone our separate ways once we reached our lockers, but with the situation we were in, we had an unspoken agreement to go home and discuss our plan.

Arnold kept looking around the car park, ready for any attack. Once we got into the car safely without incident, he relaxed slightly. But we still hadn't said a word all day. And I didn't dare to say anything to Arnold at the moment.

When we arrived home, Maria's car was already parked in the driveway. I wasn't surprised that Arnold had told her to come home early. We needed everyone to be present. This was an emergency.

As soon as we stepped through the door and saw Maria, Arnold spoke. He told her that I gave the money. He told her I kneeled in front of everyone. He told her that Brigid took the money and thrown it near the bin. He told her that Brigid saw that I wasn't afraid of her. That she didn't accept the money and gave me two options. That I chose to be her marked victim.

They both looked at me. I knew what they wanted me to say. I knew what they would have wanted me to choose. But I couldn't deny any of it. What Arnold said was the truth. This was what I knew we would disagree on. And something we would never agree on. Yes, I knew that Arnold had been afraid and nervous all day, but I also knew that he was silently angry at me.

"Why didn't you choose to cry? That would have been better!"

"And let the Ministers control our lives? Again?"

"It's better than being Brigid's marked! Do you have any idea what she could do? What she's capable of?"

"And do you think the Ministers would accept it if I made it snow? In this weather and location? Rain, storms, and hail are acceptable, but snow? They would never allow us any freedom if it ever happened."

"Are we even going to have any freedom now? With

Brigid locking us down as her target? We can't avoid her at school. We can't avoid her here."

"But we avoided the Ministers from coming into this world. We avoided you returning. We can continue with our initial plan. Nothing has changed."

Arnold stormed towards me and grabbed me by the shoulders, shaking me. "You're going to get yourself killed sooner than you think!"

I tried to remain calm. "I would have died anyway if any human got hurt from the snow." That stopped Arnold. I softened my words. "I won't die. Not until I know you're ready for the throne." He started to shake my shoulders again.

"If it was like this then I don't want it! You know what I want. I want you to-"

"Didn't you say that you wanted justice for your dad? That you wanted to reveal the truth? That you want your family name to be cleared? That you don't want Maria to be treated as a servant ever again?"

He didn't reply. But he didn't have to - we both knew what the answer was. If anything, his hands gripped tighter on my shoulders. We didn't move and kept staring at each other. Neither of us backed down.

"Arnold. Please calm down. Let's think this through." Maria spoke softly as she touched his arm. They must have spoken to one another. After a few minutes, he finally let go of my shoulders. Then he turned away from me and Maria held my hand. "Dearest, you know how we feel about this."

I nodded. I knew it too well. "I thought of something anyway."

It was like a ray of hope to them. Maria sighed in relief. "Thank goodness. I always knew you would find a way."

Maria hugged me. I snuggled in her arms like a small child. Arnold just looked at us with sad eyes. I left for my room.

As soon as I turned around the corner, I heard Arnold cry in a quiet, broken voice, "Mum… She *crawled* to get that envelope… When I saw that… My heart broke…"

Maria broke into tears, "Oh, Arnold."

"And… and then…"

I continued to my room.

I chose this path. I will protect them. No matter what.

CHAPTER TEN

Even if Brigid wanted to do something, thanks to my special privileges, she hardly saw me. And even if she did, she wouldn't be able to gain as big an audience as she'd normally have liked. She would want her first show of action to be as grand as possible. So for now I was safe. I managed to avoid her for the rest of the week. But I knew of one event that she was looking forward to.

We were in the gym again for the last dance lesson we would be required to take. I knew Brigid had been waiting for this moment because even if I wanted to escape, I wouldn't be able to. And I couldn't escape from her forever. The longer she had to wait to act, the worse she would do to the victim. I could no longer prolong it. She wouldn't do anything with the teachers around. She would have to wait until after the lesson. Despite everything, this was actually my perfect opportunity to try and talk to her.

"Okay, we're swapping out partners." The teacher, who was teaching us the waltz, stopped the music. "You've all been dancing with the same person over and over again. It's time to mix it up."

She went around the room tapping students on the shoulder and directing them. "You go with this person. And you can go here. And you can dance with him. And–" The person she paired up with me turned out to be Sasha.

What kind of fate is this?

We stared at each other until the music started to play. He took my hands and I let him. But I didn't blush or act nervous. I didn't have to play the innocent girl anymore. That, in a way, was a relief and comfort. I didn't have the time or energy to deal with him when we both knew what would happen when the song ended. I didn't have anything to say to him, but of course he wanted to talk.

"So what's your plan?"

"Why should I tell you?"

"You are one special girl. No one has ever made Brigid so angry. You must be very afraid now." I knew

Sasha would come to slap it in my face.

"I'm sorry to disappoint you, but I am not."

But he was right. I was worried. Worried that my plan wouldn't work. Worried that I'd stay as Brigid's target forever. Worried about revealing my power. But I put a smile on my face for him to see. As if everything was alright. Because I didn't want to show that kind of weakness in front of him.

"I didn't mean to," Sasha said suddenly.

I was thrown off by those words. "What do you mean?"

"I didn't mean to make you more worried than you already are."

I scoffed. "I'm not worried. Why should I be worried?"

"You're really good at hiding your emotions. But I can tell. You're worried that your plan won't go well."

I was surprised. Was he really able to read my emotions just as I was able to read everyone else's? No one was ever able to read me. Not even Maria and Arnold could see through me, and they were the closest to me. But Sasha? I always thought Sasha was a puppet, but I guess there was more to him. I have to avoid him as much as I could in the future. I looked away from him. But then a thought came to me.

"You had something to do with this, didn't you?"

"Hey, I wasn't the one who dropped the skeleton on

top of her. Hell, I wasn't the one who chose not to cry."

That was true. But now I couldn't help but think he had something to do with this. After all, he would get his revenge.

"I mean it's the perfect time for you to get back at me. Why wouldn't you take this opportunity to tell Brigid I was playing the innocent girl?"

"Because... I just wouldn't."

There was more that he didn't want to say. And that look he gave me... But I'd take his word for now. In the end, I had caused this myself.

"My plan will work."

Sasha didn't say anything for the rest of the dance. He didn't even try his usual tactics. If anything, he led the dance well enough that I lost myself in the nearly non-existent happiness that I found. It made me less nervous. It gave me energy. It made me relax. I could do this. When the dance ended, I knew this would be the start of everything.

"Well done, boys and girls. I am so proud of everyone. Thank you for attending all these dance classes. The next time I'll see you will be at the ball, breaking these moves. Everyone is dismissed." The class clapped, along with the teachers. Everyone moved to grab their bags and I waited for Arnold.

I stepped out of the gym. Brigid and her gang were

waiting for me. The sky was clear with not even a single cloud in the sky. It was as if it were mocking me.

"Long time no see, Layla!" She was so happy to see me. She had waited for this moment for a long time.

I smiled brightly in return. No more cowering. No more pretending.

I could be the person I always am in front of her from now on.

"Hi, Brigid." I crossed my arms.

She saw the movement and didn't look too happy, but she said in a cheery voice, "How have you been?" A small crowd had gathered around us. The larger crowd around the school had stopped what they were doing and stared at us from far away.

"I would like to go home."

I glimpsed a water bottle behind one of the boys next to her. I took a few steps back and tried to calm down. I knew she would bring in water as my first punishment. She didn't need to put in a lot of effort trying to scare me. I looked at Arnold. He saw what I saw. His eyes told me he was ready. I returned my gaze to Brigid. "Wouldn't you like to leave early for the day?"

"No, not really. I was hoping we could hang out for a little bit. Me and you." She waved her hand in a friendly gesture at the gap between us. But I knew that it wouldn't be just between her and me. I had a whole audience watching this show.

"If that's the case, we can have a little chat," I suggested.

"Oh? What about?"

"Something more exciting. Let's talk about boys." We were sounding like teenage girls who were best of friends.

"Before we have this chat, let's grab a drink."

And then everything happened so fast.

Brigid took a few steps back. The boy stepped forward and took the cap off the water bottle. As Brigid moved I stepped back too, and Arnold launched himself in front of me and took the blow.

Everyone around us gasped in shock. I checked myself. There was not even a single drop of water on me. Arnold must have used his powers to divert the water. I sighed in relief. Thank goodness it had worked out well.

Crouched behind Arnold, I closed my eyes and fell onto the floor. I made sure that my skin wouldn't touch the water. The floor was drier than I would have imagined. He did control the water really well. I was proud of him. Arnold touched my shoulder and I could sense his panic through his grip.

Don't worry. I'm only fake fainting. Did you forget I was supposed to be afraid of water? I'm alright. Let's leave now before anything else happens.

Arnold loosened his grip and moved the water on his skin around slowly as best as he could so that I wouldn't touch any. Then he lifted me halfway up into a sitting position with my head leaning against his shoulder.

Layla, I think you should look at this.

My eyes still closed, I looked at the scene through Arnold's eyes. I thought I would be looking at Brigid.

Never would I have imagined I would see the back of Sasha.

Standing in front of us.

Facing Brigid.

Drenched in water.

It couldn't be.

Some of the water had landed on Arnold. But the majority had gone onto Sasha. I was so shocked – I made the temperature drop around us. Not that anyone would have noticed the cold. Everyone was busy watching the scene that unfolded right in front of us. But I knew better and kept my emotions in check. The temperature turned slightly back to normal.

Was this really happening? Sasha Reynold. Second in command. Betraying Brigid. Did he know what he was doing? Why was he doing this?

A heavy silence hung in the air. Brigid and Sasha stared at each other for a long time. No one talked. No one dared to move. Everyone was frozen, waiting.

Arnold and I were unable to leave, or else we'd draw attention to ourselves. Then again, we would need to see what was happening to the very end. Because this could change everything.

"Sasha. What are you doing?" Brigid was barely audible. She was angry. So angry that her hands were shaking slightly.

"Brigid... You've gone too far this time." We couldn't see Sasha's expression, but Brigid looked like she was ready to eat him alive.

"What's that supposed to mean?"

"I meant what I said. This joke isn't funny."

"Do you know what you're doing right now?"

"If I didn't, I wouldn't be standing here."

There was another long silence.

Brigid clenched her fist. "Why are you doing this?"

"This is not right. She's afraid of water. And you know that and you're taking advantage of it. You're allergic to water too. How could you do that to another person when you know how it feels?"

Brigid didn't say anything for a while. She just kept staring at him, her eyes filled with murderous intent. Everyone in her gang fidgeted, not knowing what to do. Then she looked at my body but spoke to Sasha.

"Is this the choice that you've made?"

"Mark me."

The silence was unbearable. The shock vibrated throughout the crowd. But no one made a sound. I don't think anyone was breathing. I couldn't believe what was happening. This couldn't be real.

But then she looked at him again. "You'll wish you never said those words."

Brigid turned and stomped off with her gang in tow. All the students moved out of her way, afraid she might take her anger out on them next.

We've got to leave now. Or else Brigid might remember us.

I nodded slightly and Arnold closed the communication between us.

He put his arms around me, lifted and then carried me. I wrapped my arm around myself and rested my head against his shoulder. He made sure to only touch my clothes in case there was any water on him. Then he walked straight towards the car. I wanted to have a look at the situation behind us, so I opened my eyes as if I'd just woken up… and locked eyes with Sasha.

He stood there, soaked from head to toe, water dripping from his face. We held each other's gaze for a while. And I felt something pass between us. His gaze was determined and strong yet soft and… as if he was apologising. I don't know what I conveyed back through my eyes.

But I knew one thing. I'd escaped from Brigid and

it was thanks to him. And with that, I closed my eyes again, my thoughts conflicted.

We reached the car and Arnold skilfully opened the passenger's door and let me in. It was only when he started to drive that I finally stopped pretending. Arnold looked super happy.

"Layla, we're no longer targets. We are no longer targets!" He was bouncing in his seat.

I crossed my arms and sat there. "Yes, we are no longer targets."

Arnold laughed a little, but then he saw my face. "What's the matter?"

"I can't believe what I just witnessed. Did Sasha really stand in front of you? Did he take that blow?"

He didn't need to step out. He didn't need to defend me. He didn't need to do anything. He could have just stood in the crowd and watched, like everyone else but he didn't – he stood right in front of *us*.

"Yes, he did. I could hardly believe it myself."

"But why?" I asked myself, but Arnold answered me anyway.

"He owes us. He was the one who started this. If it hadn't been for him, none of this would have happened. We would have lived a normal life without any disruptions. So he should be the one to end it." That was true. But there should be more to it.

"There could only be three reasons. One, because I know his secret. Two, he felt sorry for me. Three, he has an ulterior motive."

"What was your plan anyway?" he asked. I looked outside at the sky without replying. It was still clear of clouds. That must have been a good omen. "Layla?"

"I was going to reveal Sasha's secret."

"You were? Why?"

"Everyone thought we committed the worse crime anyone could possibly have done to Brigid. But that's not true. There's something even worse than what I did. Something where the person who is the closest to Brigid, who she puts her trust in, betrays her. That would be the death punishment for Brigid."

And Sasha did that – on his own.

There was a chance that the plan wouldn't have worked. Brigid could have dismissed it as my desperate way to get out of the situation, and if Sasha denied it, she would have most likely believed him. It might have worked since I was going to point out the witness, but Brigid might have also dismissed that. Now, no one could know what the outcome would have been.

"Well, at least he put the plan into action," Arnold said.

It still didn't make sense why he did it though. Did he want to look like a hero by trying to save me? Was that why? Why would he try to act as a hero? Did he have an ulterior motive? But what could he possibly achieve by being Brigid's target? What would he get from me? It would make more sense if he felt sorry for me. But was Sasha capable of such an emotion?

Then I thought of the look we exchanged. I refused to believe he did it because he cared for me. He should have known that Arnold would have protected me. He didn't need to. I did not need to thank him. Anyway, he was the one who had started all of this, so he deserved it. I would never forgive him for trying to ruin my life. I could finally sigh in relief. We were no longer Brigid's target. And that was what mattered the most.

CHAPTER ELEVEN

I never would have imagined the things they would do to Sasha. I had decided it was safer for me to stay at home with Maria so I missed his opening event. But Arnold told me that when Sasha walked into school, instead of paper, they threw food garbage at him. Throughout the entire day, they poured dirty water onto him.

And by the end of the day, rumours were going around that he'd been doused in gasoline. This might be Brigid's standard of playing around, but for someone who was once on the same level and had done the same thing with the same people to end up like this... I couldn't believe it. They showed no mercy.

When I went back to school, there were days when

I witnessed Brigid doing something cruel towards him or heard from people about what had happened to him. Every time it happened, I couldn't help but wonder why Sasha chose to become a target. Was this worth it? He had looked so confident and brave at the start, but by the end of the week when I caught a glimpse of him, he'd been avoiding people and appeared slightly frightened.

In classes, Brigid and her gang would give us a glance. But they wouldn't do anything. Since they had shown they had no interest in me anymore, it was safe to take public transport again. I had been taking the car for safety reasons, but it had disrupted Arnold's practice and I never liked that. It took me forever to convince him. In the end, I had to threaten him with an order; only then did he allow me.

So I got onto the bus, and sure enough, there were only two other people on it. No student liked to take this bus. It not only took a longer route, but it also stopped at every bus stop on its way. It would be the worst bus to take for anyone in a hurry, but for me it was the safest.

Until I saw Sasha climbing on board.

Both of us were surprised. I didn't expect to see him again like this, with no one else around. I didn't expect him to be here. But if I thought about it, anyone who wanted to avoid people would take this route.

We stared at each other for a while, until Sasha started walking towards me.

He wouldn't sit right next to me, would he? I turned my head and looked out of the window. No. He couldn't possibly. We had nothing to say to each other. My mind flashed back to that day.

Maybe I do want to ask out of curiosity. But it's not worth the trouble. I would rather it remain a mystery than create trouble for myself by speaking to him first.

He walked past me and sat at the back. That worked well for me.

Each time the bus stopped, neither Sasha nor I got off. In the end, only the two of us were left. I wouldn't have been surprised if he'd tried to talk to me eventually. Whether for revenge or if he wanted something.

That's the way humans are.

They act so that they can take what they want. He must have regretted what he'd done that day. So now he must have wanted to change his circumstances. A buzzer sounded on the bus. This must be Sasha's stop. This was also a good opportunity for him to say something to me. But he got off without a single word.

"I saw Sasha on the bus."

Maria looked over at me from the driver's seat. She'd

picked me up at the usual bus stop, which was in the residential area, away from the main roads. "Really?"

"Don't mention a word to Arnold. Or else he'll worry for no reason."

"Was that an order?"

I gave her a stern look.

"I was joking. Did he do or say anything?"

I shook my head.

"Well, that is a surprise. Brigid must have been really angry with him if she hasn't changed her target."

That was true. Brigid tended to get bored if she stayed with one target for too long. But Sasha had betrayed Brigid. This was a special case.

"But since he is and I'm not the target, our life is back to how it was before."

He hadn't said anything to me on the bus. That must mean he didn't want to have anything to do with me. If that was the case, it was as if nothing ever happened. Everything was back to normal.

"If I told you–" I looked at Maria, who seemed a little careful with her words. "–that I'm starting to feel sorry for the boy, what would you think?"

I looked out the window.

"I would say, don't. He deserved it."

"But he did help you."

"As he should."

"He took the trouble upon himself. He's been suffering alone. Even if he did play the bully, didn't he try to help all the other people who have suffered? He's not entirely bad. Don't you feel sorry for him, even a little?"

"No. Not at all. He chose to, so it's his own fault."

"It doesn't change the fact that he did it for you."

"For me or for himself?"

"You don't know that. You should try asking him. Aren't you curious to know why?"

"I am. But I don't want to ask. As long as our life is back to normal, isn't that what matters the most?"

"I think you should have a word with him at least."

"I don't need to." But that sounded rude, so I rephrased it: "I don't think we need to."

"Layla, you're being awfully stubborn about this. Are you afraid of his answer?"

"No, I'm not. Are you trying to tell me something?"

"Okay, okay, I'll drop the topic."

We sat in a comfortable silence for the rest of the drive.

I wasn't afraid of his answer. It was more that I wanted to test him. To see if he wanted something from me. To see how he would handle everything. To figure out why he did step in. The bus had been the perfect opportunity for him to make a move. No one we knew was around. And he would have had enough time to talk to me. But he didn't.

* * *

Another week passed. Every day, Sasha would suffer. Every day, we would catch the same bus. And every day we wouldn't speak a word to each other. It became a comfortable routine for me.

I was walking to the bus stop, having left school early as usual. I reached into my bag for my phone… and it wasn't there. Arnold was always nagging me to check for my phone, but I hadn't listened to him today.

I turned and walked as fast as I could towards my locker. The bell would ring to signal the end of school very soon, so I'd have to hurry. I honestly didn't see the need for a mobile phone when I was always with them, nearly every second of my life. But it was better to be safe than sorry.

As I entered the school, I heard voices from near the locker area. I stopped in my tracks and rested my back against the wall. They didn't stop talking, so I guessed they didn't hear my arrival. Looked like I would need to take the long way around to my locker.

"Yes, I did."

I recognised that voice. I took a quick peek and rested my back against the wall again. Sure enough, it was Sasha, talking to a girl.

They must have skipped class to meet each other here. But it didn't seem like they were having a good conversation. I didn't recognise the girl. Then again, I wouldn't have remembered her anyway. There was the sound of books being thrown onto the floor.

"Did you honestly think you were helping me back then? You're completely wrong! Thanks to you and her gang, no one has ever lived peacefully. I hope you rot in hell!"

"I am sorry."

There was a long heavy silence between them.

"Do you not have a conscience? My life is ruined because of you."

I didn't want to hear anymore. Time was running out, so I set off on the long route to my locker. From my understanding of that conversation, she used to be a victim of Brigid, and Sasha had tried to help. But she was not grateful for it.

I rushed to my locker and grabbed my phone. As soon as I was out of the school building, the bell rang. What good timing. I walked faster to the bus stop so that I wouldn't bump into anyone else.

The bus wasn't there yet. I sat on the bench and finally caught my breath. Arnold would be laughing at my stamina right now. My human body just wasn't fit to do any physical activity.

My thoughts strayed to Sasha. I didn't think he would ever apologise. Was he trying to redeem himself? Did he finally see the mistakes that he'd made and want to... change? Was that why he helped me? Because he no longer thought it was right? That was impossible.

Humans never change.

The bus must have been late because even Sasha came to wait. We ignored each other like we usually did. I didn't want to think about what happened earlier anymore, so I reached for my bag. As I opened it, I accidentally dropped my towel.

The wind picked it up and it flew into the puddle of muddy water near Sasha's feet. He retrieved it and looked at me. Then he walked towards me with the wet towel in his hands.

What was he doing? Didn't he know I was afraid of water? Why was he walking towards me? He should have left my wet towel where it was.

"Here."

He offered me my towel, waiting for me to accept it. I stared at him for a long time. He must have felt awkward because he put the towel next to me on the bench. "Sorry." He started to walk away, but I had a bad feeling.

"Why did you hand me my wet towel?"

He stopped. My gaze stayed on his back as I waited

for him to reply. It felt like forever before he did.

"If I told you I might know something, what would you do?" He slowly turned around. He looked worried.

So I told him, "We need to talk."

* * *

During the bus ride, we sat separately. I had told him to follow me, and so far he was. This couldn't be happening. It made no sense. How could he have known? No, he couldn't have found out. It was just impossible.

When the bus neared my stop, I pressed the signal button. I got off and Sasha did the same. I sat on the bench and waited for Maria. Sasha sat next to me, not saying a word. But I could tell he was waiting for something to happen.

Maria pulled up. She was surprised to see a boy in the same uniform as me, and not only that but also sitting right next to me. I climbed into the car and sat next to Maria. Sasha took the hint and took the back seat. Now she was really shocked.

"Who do we have here?"

"Hi, Layla's mum."

"Mum, this is Sasha."

She didn't bother to hide her shock. Maria looked from me to him, her mouth open. She composed herself and said, "I didn't know we were having a guest today."

"We needed to talk. I thought you should know as well."

Now Maria looked worried as she drove to our house. She took a look at me and I smiled back at her. She knew what that meant and focused on the road ahead.

I was too calm for something this dangerous to be happening. This could change everything again and even worse. But in all honesty, I wasn't as afraid as I should have been. In the end, I didn't want to let Sasha know how much it would affect us since he could read me better than he should. For now, I needed him to follow us home.

"Arnold..." Maria started.

"...will come home after," I finished.

I didn't want Arnold to be here just yet. I could only imagine what he would do if he was. After that, no one in the car spoke for the entire ride.

Sometimes I would look at Sasha in the mirror. He would either be on his phone or staring out of the window. Maria might be panicking, but I was curious. He had no idea what he'd got himself into. We arrived at our house and went inside.

"Make yourself comfortable. Would you like anything to drink?" Maria asked.

"No thank you, ma'am."

Maria ignored Sasha and went into the kitchen. She

must have been very nervous. I stood with my arms crossed while Sasha sat on the couch opposite to me.

I rushed towards him, formed an ice sword in a flash and pointed it right in front of his face.

Cold air radiated from the sword. The blade wasn't as straight as I hoped it would be. It was more like a branch from a tree. At least it wasn't melting. With my powers, this would have to do. He didn't need to know that. But it must be working.

Because he didn't move. He sat very still and stared at my sword. He stayed silent. I could see the truth sinking in. He hadn't realised what this would involve. How much trouble it would bring him. He was messing with the wrong people from the very beginning. His eyes slowly filled with fear. He couldn't run or hide.

I smiled sweetly.

"You will answer everything I ask and you will only give me the truth." He nodded. "How did you know I wasn't afraid of water?"

"On the day when you offered the money to Brigid, I happened to see you that night. I didn't think it was you at first, but then I saw Arnold and knew it had to be you. Arnold was searching the area, so I hid. I was curious what you guys were up to. Arnold disappeared into the water and then somehow you looked different and then you walked into the water despite being 'afraid' of it.

That's when I knew that there was something more to your story."

"And then what happened?"

"I didn't see you or Arnold come back for a while even though I waited. And since you guys were taking so long and I couldn't see anything in the water, I just left."

He knew that long ago? "Why were you out so late?"

"I was at a party nearby. I came out to the beach for some air and that was when I saw you."

Brigid must have thrown a party to celebrate. We should have known. We were careless. "Was there anyone else?"

"I was alone."

"Did you tell anyone?" This was the most important question.

"No."

We went silent. I narrowed my eyes at him.

"How am I supposed to trust that you didn't tell a soul?"

"If I did tell anyone, it would have been Brigid. And if Brigid knew, then she wouldn't have used the water bottle to scare you."

That made sense. But he was calm, too calm for my liking when he answered me. He was scared. He was very careful with every word he was saying. The wheels in his head were turning with each question. But for him

114

to show a calm face and for his voice to come out so even, made me slightly worried.

"Why didn't you? I thought you didn't like me. You could have used it against me and had your revenge."

"I didn't understand what was happening. How could I use it against you? But then I thought if you were going to such lengths to hide this secret, it must have been very important."

I gave him a questioning look.

"Please believe me. Or you can do whatever you like to me."

I smirked. He had just been sitting still, watching my every movement. It was the first sign that gave away how scared he was. I pointed the ice sword closer to his face. "Aren't you afraid that I will kill you?"

"I am. But I believe that if I give you whatever you want, you'll spare my life." He was right, but I wouldn't be able to kill him anyway.

"Did you help me because you found out my secret?"

"It was the right thing to do."

"Was that all? No other reason?"

"I also felt guilty since I found out. And I... wanted to gain your trust and forgiveness."

We were quiet for a while, just staring at each other.

"Why would you want that?"

"Because I wanted a friend. To be your friend."

I couldn't believe what I was hearing. I was going to tell him so, but then I really looked at him. He seemed genuine when he said all those words. But that still didn't lessen my suspicions of him. "Why me?"

"I wanted to start over and I thought you would be the best person. You're the only one who could tell if I was lying or not. I trust you."

A human trying to change? Impossible.

"You said earlier that I can do anything to you. Do you even know what that means?" I moved my arm and touched the sword against his face. He shivered. "Are you sure you can handle anything?"

He didn't reply so I spoke again. "What if I told you I want to erase your memory?"

He looked so shocked yet so calm. I had wanted him to be frightened. So scared that he would cry and beg for his life. But he hadn't. I admit I was fairly impressed. But I knew he wasn't going to cooperate. He didn't really have a choice. I was going to erase his memory either way.

It would have been easier if he'd followed instructions. If he thought he could make it out with his memory intact, then there was nothing we could do about it. We would have to do this the hard way. I took a step towards him.

"Yes, you can."

I froze for a moment. He surprised me. I honestly didn't think he would have agreed. He knew now that I was not human. That I was a being with the ability to wield water. So how did he know I wouldn't hurt him? What made him think that I wouldn't kill him off? Did he trust me enough to agree to this?

"Aren't you afraid you won't even remember your own name?"

"I trust that you only want to protect your secret and that you would only erase what you need to."

Smart boy, for him to see the situation so clearly. No wonder he was Brigid's second in command. At least this made things a lot easier. I made my ice sword turn into bubbles.

"Alright then. Maria, could you please come in."

Maria came in from the kitchen. I extended my hand and she took it. I replayed my memories of the bus stop event as best as possible, for Maria to see.

Please erase this memory as well, I told her through my touch.

She nodded.

"Since I won't remember anything about you anymore." Maria and I looked at him as he spoke. "Will you be my friend afterwards?"

This person kept surprising me. It was becoming unsettling. He looked me in the eye, unwavering. His jaw set with determination. I stared right back at him.

Was he in his right mind? I didn't want anything to do with him after all of this. Let alone become friends with a human. He must have read the answer on my face, because he looked away and said, "Never mind."

"Close your eyes," Maria told him. Sasha hesitated, but then he did. "Now remember exactly what you saw that night."

Maria transformed into her true form and placed her hand on his head. Sasha shivered but didn't open his eyes. Her hands would have been cold. But he must have been afraid as well. Maria closed her eyes, keeping her hand still as Sasha's body slowly relaxed.

It was the first time I had witnessed a memory being erased. I hoped that it would be the last. Maria looked at him with complete focus. Hours went by, and then it must have ended because Sasha collapsed onto the couch. Maria sighed and transformed back into her human form. She turned and looked at me.

"What are we going to do now?"

"Now we can call Arnold."

* * *

"Why didn't you call me the second you found out he knew your identity?!"

"He doesn't know who I am."

We were all in the living room with Sasha unconscious on the couch. Arnold and Maria were near him, while I sat on the opposite couch sipping on my water. We agreed that it was better for me to stay away from Sasha in case my powers became unstable and I decided to kill him in his sleep.

"Are you sure you erased his memory correctly?" Arnold asked, shaking Sasha quite violently.

We looked at Maria. "Yes. I erased the one he was thinking about. It would just be a memory of him walking to and from the beach. Any memory related will slowly erase itself. He shouldn't remember any of it by the time he wakes up in a couple of days."

Arnold nodded and then turned to me. "Are you sure he didn't tell anyone?"

"It's been a while now. And nothing has happened to us, so it's safe to say no one else knows about me."

"Are you sure the Ministers don't know about this?"

"If they did, they would have already come and knocked on the door."

"Are you sure?"

I got up and took Arnold's shaking hands. "Arnold, please calm down. Everything is okay now. We're okay."

"Are you sure?" he asked. I nodded. He slowly started to relax. "He's the first human to suspect."

"I know."

119

We all stared at Sasha's unconscious body again. Then Arnold said, "What were the odds that Sasha was out that night?"

"It was just bad luck and bad timing," I said.

"Even so, I should've checked carefully."

"He was hiding. He purposely didn't let you find him. What could you have done? We'll be careful next time." I smiled and tugged his arm to try to make him feel better, but he kept going.

"He could have figured out you were the Winter Queen."

"He wouldn't have, from just that. He doesn't know that I control the weathers, let alone that I'm the Queen."

"How can you be so calm about this?"

"I have to be. I have no choice." He froze. I gave him a small smile. "You know I'll always find a solution to everything. We're safe."

Arnold nodded and smiled. So many things could have happened. But for once, something had worked in our favour. Sasha hadn't told anyone and he hadn't figured out my identity. That's what mattered right now. We'd hidden it very well for so long and he was the first human to have sensed something wrong. But I'd make sure he was the last one.

"She made an ice sword and threatened him."

Arnold's eyes widened at Maria's statement. I gave

Maria a look. I couldn't believe she'd betrayed me.

"I wanted to scare him so that he would work with us."

"That would have been dangerous! What if you'd accidentally hurt him?"

"If we were going to erase his memory, he needed to realise just how bad the situation he was in."

"He knows you have powers!"

"And now he's forgotten them. That was all in my plan." Arnold was about to say something else, but I cut him off. "You can argue with me later. Let's get Sasha home."

"Okay, but we are going to have a serious talk afterwards."

CHAPTER TWELVE

Arnold knew where Sasha lived, so he dropped him off at his house. No one was home, so he had to open the door with Sasha's keys. He left him in bed. He said that he never wanted to do that ever again.

A few days later, Sasha returned to school and it was as if nothing had happened to him. Brigid punished him even more than usual, but that was to be expected. Sasha suffered. On a few occasions, I caught him looking at me. It was as if he wanted me to talk to him. But he didn't say a word to me, even though we caught the same bus. He didn't approach me either. We could confirm – he had forgotten everything.

I kept my distance anyway. Even if he had forgotten

everything, I knew that he would still want to be "friends" with me. And I did not want that to happen. Now that I knew why he helped me, there was no reason to pay any attention to him anymore.

"He's actually not as bad a person as I imagined him to be," Maria said as she picked me up from the usual spot.

"Sasha?"

"Yeah."

"Why would you think that?"

"He helped you evade Brigid's target. He was willing to erase his memory." I was about to speak, but Maria continued, "Yes, I know he deserves it since he was the one who started everything. But he's willing to change for the better. Isn't that the most important thing?"

I didn't reply.

"He could have revealed your secret to everyone, but he didn't. Don't you feel sorry for him now? Shouldn't we at least thank him even just a little bit?"

I didn't reply to that either.

* * *

Nearly a month had passed. Winter had ended and spring was starting. There were days that were still cold, but the flowers were in full bloom. Sasha was still the target. Nothing had changed. Every day he would be punished in a different way. Arnold and I kept our heads low and away from her group.

The last class of the day was gym. Our entire class had to do a three-kilometre run around the school block. As I was exempt from participating in any sports event, I sat on the grass and did my school homework. Brigid was also exempt from sports events, but she had left class early and gone home. Arnold ran past me with a smile. He must have been enjoying the workout. It was another way for him to keep fit. Sasha ran past with a grim expression on his face.

Everyone was finishing their final lap. Arnold ran an extra lap, prolonging his workout. There was a group of boys near me that had finished early. They were whispering to each other, but I could hear them clearly.

"I think it's a good idea."

"Okay, so when Sasha comes around, we'll ask him to come to the toilets with us. Then we can beat the crap out of him and leave."

The boys snickered and talked about something else. I didn't want to hear any more, so I packed away my books and stood up to leave. I excused myself from the teachers. I would leave a note for Arnold and head for the bus early.

As I approached the school gate, Sasha came running towards me. He was sweating profusely, and his breathing was ragged. It seemed like he was pushing himself. He saw me but didn't say anything as he ran past. Normally people would run in pairs or a group. He was the only person running by himself.

Running towards a group of people who would hurt him.

"Sasha."

I turned around to look at him. He had stopped and was resting his hands on his knees, catching his breath. He looked at me, waiting for me to say something. I didn't want to admit it, but Maria was right. I did owe him at least a thank you.

I never liked to owe anyone anything.

I should help him but hadn't thought it through when I called his name. I didn't know how to start. In the far-off distance, I could see a group of boys running towards us. They were getting closer with each passing second. I didn't want to be seen alone with Sasha.

Maybe he saw my hesitation or he knew what I was thinking because he started to walk towards the gym. I went the other way, past the group of people, and walked into the other gym entrance. When we met up again, he turned towards me.

"Did you want to say something?"

He had his hands on his hips and looked impatient. What kind of attitude was that? Now I wished I hadn't spoken to him. At least I wouldn't owe him anything after this.

"I just wanted to let you know that there is a group of boys from Brigid's gang planning something that would hurt you if you ran to the oval. So it's best if you skip the rest of the class."

I'd finished what I had to say so I turned my back on him and started to walk away.

"Is that all you wanted to tell me?"

I turned around to face him again. His face bore an expression of disbelief like he was expecting something else.

"Is there something *you* want to say?"

Sasha opened his mouth but then closed it. He sighed. "You know what, forget about it."

I didn't say anything else as I watched him grab his gym bag and head towards the bathrooms. How rude! I really should have left him alone. I left the gym and continued towards my locker.

He had definitely wanted to say something. What could he want to talk to me about? His memory had been erased. I thought back to the event that started all of his misery. Did he want to talk about that?

Before the school bell rang, I headed to my usual bus stop and there was Sasha already sitting on the bench. I didn't want to go near him, so I stayed standing near the end of the bench. He got up and walked to the bus stop sign. If that was his way of giving me the seat, I didn't take it.

The bus arrived and I hopped on first and sat down. I reached into my bag for my phone. As I pulled it out, it slipped from my hand. I leaned down to get it, but another pair of hands grabbed it. I looked up, straight into Sasha's eyes. We both straightened right away. He handed me my phone, then realised what he was doing and set it on the seat right next to me. We stared at each other again.

"Are you going to sit down or hold up the line?" One of the familiar faces that took this bus stood behind Sasha, his arms crossed. Sasha looked behind the guy at the empty bus.

"Sorry, I didn't realise I was holding everyone up." Sasha sat in the seat in front of me. The guy glared at him and walked to the back of the bus. I took out my towel and wiped my phone down.

Sasha stood up.

"Wait."

He waited for me. Maybe this was a good way to test him. Just to make sure he'd forgotten everything. But I didn't know how to start this. It was the second time that day that I hadn't thought through what I should do. What was wrong with me? I blamed Maria for planting thoughts in my head.

Suddenly Sasha was sitting right next to me. I stared at him while he took his phone and wired earphones out of his bag. He was waiting for me. Because he knew what I was thinking. I stared out the window into the bright, cloudy sky. There was a long silence.

"Is there something wrong?" he said.

I looked at him and asked, "Why did you help?"

"Your phone was on the floor. I thought you might want a hand."

I looked away again. There was no point discussing it any further if he was going to act this way. He knew I was referring to his "heroic" save. I wished it wasn't so bright today.

"It was the right thing to do."

I froze for a second. That was the exact thing he'd said before his memories were erased. I studied him. Judging from his reaction, he didn't think much of it. He didn't remember. He really didn't remember anything. Then it must be the real reason, for him to say it twice. I narrowed my eyes.

"And you know what the right thing to do is?"

Now he narrowed his eyes at me. "Maybe you're right. I did do the wrong thing. I shouldn't have helped you. I should have left you to be Brigid's target."

He went back to staring out the window. What I

said wasn't the nicest thing to say. He did after all divert Brigid's attention. He also chose to give up his memory. But that didn't change how I felt towards him.

He looked at me again. "Do I really seem that bad?"

I raised an eyebrow. "Do you want me to be honest?"

"Is it impossible that I would want to become a better person?"

I thought back to the locker room and the conversation Sasha had with that girl. And all the things Arnold had told me about him. Sasha may have taken part in the bullying, but he'd also tried to help the victims out in a way no one else noticed.

Even when the entire group took it too far, he would somehow try to pull everyone back, to stop the worst from happening. It didn't change the fact that what he did was wrong. But was that trying to be better?

"No. It's not impossible," I said quietly.

But was it even possible? For a human to want to become better? Humans would never change. I just didn't believe him. I didn't believe in humans. They were manipulative, cunning, dishonest, cynical, unfaithful, disloyal and so many other bad terms that I could use. They always thought they were right and never wrong. Look at Brigid.

Why would they want to change for the better when they thought their life was so perfect? Why should I trust them when they had ruined my life? I stopped my thoughts and took slow, deep breaths.

Calm down. Don't get annoyed over this, calm down.

The people on the bus had been getting off one by one at the stops, as usual. The last person hopped off, leaving us alone with the bus driver.

"I know what it feels like," he said. He was staring straight ahead. Then he turned towards me. His eyes were filled with sadness. That look kept me quiet. I just listened. "To be a victim of bullying."

I never thought there would come a day when I would be sitting here listening to Sasha Reynold's life story. But to hear the words from his own mouth…

"Back in primary school, I was really popular with the girls. All the guys were jealous."

I rolled my eyes.

"You were already arrogant as a kid."

He grinned at that.

"At first, I thought they were just jokes. You know how small kids are. But then they resorted to physical and mental attacks. They would kick me, punch me, lock me up and even strip me." He paused for a second. "And the worst part was that everyone knew what was going on, but no one did a thing."

"But isn't that the same thing you did to the others here? That doesn't justify your actions."

"At least I tried to help them afterwards. Do you see any of the bullies ever apologising for what they did? Do you see them regret their decision?"

He was right. People who are superior go on with their life as if nothing happened. Whereas the people who are affected are still living in their nightmares.

"You're still the worst. To be bullied and then to bully others even when you knew how it felt."

"I did feel bad. I did feel guilty. I felt like a horrible human being. But at the same time, I didn't want to be a victim again. I didn't want to be weak anymore. Surely you know how it feels to be powerless."

I didn't answer him.

He continued, "For the six years of primary school, I endured it all. I wanted to end my life so many times."

I never thought Sasha would want to end his life. So I gently asked, "Why didn't you?"

"I didn't want to lose. Not to them. Not to myself. I was sure that other people who'd been through what I had survived. I wanted to be a part of the survivor team, I guess. Anyway, I was sure other people were having harder times than I ever did. So I told myself never to be weak again."

"And you thought by becoming a bully that would make you strong?"

"I thought I would have control. That I would have

power. But I recently realised that's not the answer. That's why I wanted to stop everything before I could no longer stop."

"Why did you choose to stop now?"

"You were the only one who was never afraid of Brigid. I liked how you stood your ground."

He gave me a lopsided grin and I gave him another eyebrow raise.

"Okay, at first, I admit I wanted to see how long it would take you to crack under the pressure. Till then, no one had lasted as long as you had and hadn't begged for Brigid's mercy. I found that admirable. Because it was something I could have done but didn't have the courage to do in the beginning. I like your courage."

The words were left hanging in the air between us, sinking in. I'd never received a positive remark from a human, so I didn't know how to respond. Instead, I thought back to the story he told me.

My deductions were right when I first accused him of being a victim. At least he confirmed it. It made sense why he was nice to his victims. The question had been answered. The reason why he chose to be the victim that day instead of me. He could only have felt sorry for me. Like how he felt for all of his other victims. He was slowly trying to make things right. I guess… there was a tiny bit of hope for humanity, after all. The bus drove on and we sat in comfortable silence.

"But I never knew being Brigid's marked was this hard." He shook his head. "I guess I'll have to endure until she finds a new target."

I snorted. "We both know that's not going to happen."

"That's alright, it's better this way. I'll endure it. I kinda deserved it."

He'd lasted longer than I would have thought. It didn't seem like he'd given up yet. He wasn't running away. He was facing it head-on. And he was accepting his punishment for all the things he'd done. He knew he deserved it. That was something I considered admirable. The bus drew closer to my stop. I stood up and he moved for me.

"At least you admitted your mistake. Not many people would be able to do that. So... that's really brave of you too."

He didn't say anything else so I got off the bus. I was having the strangest day. What had gotten into me? Saying these kinds of things. And to Sasha, of all people. I shook my head and turned to sit on the bench, nearly walking into Sasha himself. I stepped back and looked up at him. He gazed down at me with one of his hands in his pockets.

"What are you doing?"

"This is your fault. You made me tell you my life

story, so I missed my stop."

"That is not my fault at all!" I couldn't believe he'd got off the bus with me. "What are you going to do?"

"I'll need directions."

I sighed. "Where do you need to go?"

"To your heart."

A light breeze passed between us that had nothing to do with me. He had a gentle smile as he stared at me with an expression I didn't understand. I would have completely ignored him and changed the topic, but I couldn't do anything except stare back.

"Layla?"

I turned around. Maria rolled down her window. She had parked on the side of the street. She must have thought there was something going on between us because she was smiling. "Who is this?"

"Hello, ma'am. I'm Sasha Reynold."

"Hi Sasha, I'm Layla's mum." She glanced at me then and smiled even brighter. At least she was acting as if this was the first time she'd met him. "Are you coming over for dinner?"

My eyes widened. *Maria!*

"I'm invited to dinner?" He glanced at me and smiled.

I glared at Maria to tell her to stop doing what I knew she was doing. "No, I was thinking we could kindly drop him off home," I said.

"She must have forgotten to mention it!" She completely ignored me and addressed Sasha. "I wanted to thank you for defending my daughter. She told me all about it. If you aren't busy, would you like to join us for dinner tonight?"

I turned to him and gave a meaningful look. *Say no. Tell her no.*

"I would love to."

I closed my eyes. *Why?!*

I opened my eyes. Maria looked like she was going to jump with joy. I turned to face him and glared. He knew that I didn't want this. But he gave me a smile to say everything would be alright. "So, what's for dinner?"

* * *

We drove to the grocery shops. I had always avoided such crowded places, where there were so many risks. I touched my hand against Maria's where it rested on the gear stick and argued silently throughout the entire ride.

This was a mistake.

This was a bad idea.

What if Sasha finds out my identity again?

She said that as long as I stuck close to her, I would be safe. I shouldn't be worried if Maria was the one protecting me. She was the reason why Arnold was so strong. I argued even more, but she wasn't hearing any of it. I wouldn't be able to change her mind unless I commanded her to, but I never wanted to force Maria to do anything against her will. So I gave in and followed Maria down every aisle, with Sasha pushing the trolley.

I've never been to a grocery store. I was surprised the place was bustling with life. The smell of fruit and vegetables was overpowering. I was amazed by all the food. There were so many things on the shelves that I'd never known existed. It was interesting.

I was even more surprised that Maria knew what she was buying. She must have wanted to find a reason to make these human recipes. She had finally found a victim. They could not stop talking to each other. Asking questions and making jokes.

Maria kept asking what Sasha would like to eat, and he must have had some knowledge of cooking because he picked all the ingredients. At this rate, they would become best friends. I wanted to go home.

When we finally got to the house, Sasha helped Maria carry the groceries in. I could tell that made her like him even more. I didn't want to watch any longer, so I went into the living room, sat on the couch, and started on my homework. Maria stayed in the kitchen preparing food while Sasha sat on the couch opposite me. It was very odd to see him sitting there. In the same place he had lost his memories.

"You can take your leave now, while it's not too late."

"I think I'll stick around for dinner."

"Don't you have your own place to have dinner?"

"No, not really." We were silent for a moment. I guess he really was not that close to his family. "I really like Maria."

I couldn't believe they were already on a first-name basis. "And I don't like you being here right now."

"I know, and I'm really enjoying it. Maybe a tour around?"

I glared at him. "No."

"Come on. Let me see your room."

"Definitely not."

He stood up and walked to a door. "Maybe it's this room."

I threw my workbook down and jumped up. "Don't you dare!"

But he didn't get the chance, because Arnold came in through the front door. He stopped right in his tracks and stared at us. Then he walked out of the house and a few seconds later came back in and stared again.

"Don't worry buddy, you're in the right house."

Arnold closed the door. "This does sound like the almighty Sasha."

He looked like he was ready to kick Sasha out of the house. I definitely agreed with him and was going to tell him to do so, when a shout came from the kitchen: "Your mum is in the kitchen. Arnold, I need you to help me so could you please come over."

Arnold bolted for the kitchen without a single word, leaving me alone with Sasha again. I could imagine the argument they were most likely having. I wanted to say a few words too, but I wasn't allowed in the kitchen right then.

"No tours allowed. We should do our homework while we wait for them shall we?"

Sasha shrugged. Then we sat on the floor and opened our books on the coffee table. Sasha quietly wrote his answers down while I stared at my book. Even though I'd suggested the idea, the only class we had with each other was chemistry and it was my weakest subject. Sasha noticed my hesitance and *gladly* volunteered to help me.

And teased me about it.

"How do you not know this? It's the easiest thing in the world."

I was starting to feel embarrassed even when I shouldn't. "I just don't."

"Arnold must have been tutoring you if don't even know how to solve this question."

He was right. Arnold would always help me when it came to chemistry. Sometimes I would just copy his answers. I barely passed the subject but I excelled in all the other classes and that was the deal with the Ministers. I just had to excel in school didn't mean I need to excel in *all* my classes.

"If you don't want to help, then don't bother." I tried to snatch away my book, but Sasha held on tight.

"I didn't say I wouldn't help. I'm just saying how bad you are."

"I am not that bad."

"You're right. There isn't a word in the dictionary for how good you look."

I was ready to kill this boy right here right now, but after what seemed like an eternity, Maria and Arnold came out with the food. I stood up in a heartbeat, walked to the table and sat down. Sasha followed and sat right next to me. I glared at him, but he just smiled back. So I turned my head and ignored him.

There were already three plates of food on the table. But the food kept coming… and coming… and coming… and in the end the entire table was filled with food. I couldn't even see the surface.

There were dishes I recognised like pasta, chicken, steak, and some I'd never seen before. I stared at the amount of food, then at Maria, who looked so proud, and then at Sasha, who looked flustered.

"Did you make all this? In an hour?" Sasha asked.

Maria nodded vigorously.

I gave Arnold a meaningful look. Why hadn't he stopped her? He raised one eyebrow as if to say he didn't try.

"I hope you enjoy it. It's mostly all for you."

Sasha must have seen everyone's plate size because they were tiny. We could eat human food, but it was something we didn't enjoy as much. "We have small appetites," Maria explained in response to Sasha's questioning look.

"There's so much food. How am I supposed to finish all of this?"

"You can always take it home. Tell me which dishes you like and we'll put them in a container later. Let's eat, shall we?"

We sat there eating quietly, listening to Maria talking about her day since hers were always much more exciting and interesting – even hilarious. Arnold was silent at first but eventually, he contributed and laughed in the end. That didn't stop him from constantly watching Sasha's every movement.

Every time Sasha wanted to try a new dish, Maria would get it for him and then ask him a million questions. I tried not to make fun of him as Maria continued to baby him. It was amusing to see him being flustered by Maria.

But by the end of dinner, I was impressed by Sasha.

He had eaten at least half of the food. Some plates were completely clean. He liked most of them, which surprised me – Maria could *actually* cook human food. She must have been so happy since she'd always loved to cook.

"Wow. I don't think I've ever eaten this much in my entire life." Sasha sat back and groaned.

"Don't worry. I'll pack this all up for you." Maria started clearing the table.

"Wait, you don't need–" Maria had already grabbed the closest three plates to her and walked into the kitchen.

"Looks like you won't need to worry about food for a week," I said.

"More like a month." But then his tone became less sarcastic and he even smiled when he said, "But it was nice."

Sasha started grabbing plates, as did Arnold and I. Once the table was cleared, Sasha offered to stay longer to help me with my homework, but we glared at him so he said he'd go home instead. We stood near the kitchen as he was handed a huge bag of food containers.

"You don't need to give me back the containers," Maria stated.

"Of course–"

"I don't need them." Maria waved her hand,

dismissing him.

Sasha looked at the bag and then at Maria. "Thank you."

"Okay, let's drive you home."

Sasha was surprised by the offer. So were Arnold and I.

Arnold folded his arms. "He doesn't need it."

"You cooked me dinner and you're driving me home? No, that's fine. I'll grab a taxi."

"But–"

"It's fine. Really. You've done a lot for me already. I can't ask for more than that."

"No, I'm the one who has to thank you. For looking after our Layla."

"No, it's something I should do," Sasha answered.

Arnold and I exchanged a look while Maria smiled. "I still think we should drop you off."

"Don't worry, I've already called for one. It should be here any second now." I don't think I'd ever heard Sasha be so polite.

"Okay then, if you really insist. Thank you for staying for dinner. I hope to see you soon. Layla, could you please walk him out?"

Arnold made to walk with me, but Maria pulled him back. "You have to help me wash the dishes. Bye Sasha!"

And then she dragged Arnold away and they

disappeared into the kitchen. I sighed and shook my head. It was so obvious what she was trying to do. I was tempted to walk straight to my room and ignore him, but someone had to lock the door, so we started walking to the front door.

"Is your family always like this?"

Maria was definitely more excited than usual, and Arnold was more silent. But I nodded anyway.

"It must be fun every day."

I was actually surprised when I heard that. When I thought about it, every day *was* fun. Despite the situation we were in, where I was always worried. I was always careful. I was always planning. I never took the time to appreciate the happy times that did happen when I was around Arnold and Maria. They were the ones who made my life more enjoyable, more *bearable* than it would have been. I pondered on that as we walked out.

"Did you actually like the food?" I asked.

"Some of the dishes were really nice. The others… Let's just say they were interesting."

I smiled at that. That was the Maria I knew. We sat on the doorstep while we waited for the car. The streets were empty. I looked up at the sky. There were no clouds, so the night sky was shining with more stars than usual. Then I noticed that Sasha was staring at me.

"What?"

"You smiled."

I dropped the smile. "And?"

"Are you not the girl with the beautiful smile?"

He gave me a playful grin. I rolled my eyes and looked down the street, hoping the car would get here faster. "Make sure that you finish the food. Maria made that much because she was very grateful to you."

"What about you? Are you grateful?"

I didn't answer right away. I knew what he was referring to. I still believed I didn't owe him anything. But I did owe him at least a word of gratitude.

"Thank you."

I looked him right in the eye and said it. I meant those words. We held each other's gaze. A warm, gentle breeze passed between us. He flashed me a smile.

"Bet it's nice to have a family like this. I've never seen you smile before. I'd like to see you smile more."

I was about to say something when his ride pulled into our driveway. "Alright, I'll see you at school."

Sasha hopped into the car and it drove away. I tried to process the last thing he said to me.

Does he think... we're friends?

CHAPTER THIRTEEN

I went back inside the house. I should have known what was going to happen. I could hear Arnold and Maria from the entrance so I closed the door quickly and walked towards them.

"Did you forget about our plan? This could be the moment we've been waiting for!" I could tell how excited Maria was.

"I know... But Sasha Reynold..." answered Arnold.

"And so? He's changed! And the only one that would want to be friends with her. It's the perfect opportunity."

"I can't trust him with my life."

I said as I walked into the kitchen, where Maria was controlling water to wash the dishes whilst standing face to face with Arnold. They both turned to look at me. Arnold looked triumphant and Maria looked defeated at my words. But Maria wasn't going to give up easily.

"But he's the perfect human. He apologised and he's slowly changing to become better. Can't you see?"

"I can see that he's still a human and that means when he sees an opportunity to save himself, he will."

"But he didn't. He chose to take your place." I didn't have anything to say to that. Maria continued, "I know we can trust this human."

"We can't change his nature."

"Who says? If he can change his attitude and values, why can't he go against his nature? This is the perfect opportunity for us." Maria turned to Arnold. "Think about it. Do you want to go along with Layla's plan? Wouldn't this be better?"

I also knew what Arnold's train of thought would be. "That's true… Even if he did get us into trouble in the past, maybe he could help us now. We could change our plans-"

"We don't need to change plans though. Why would we need to?" I said.

It must have been my tone of voice and what I'd said that made Arnold move, because now he stood in front of me. "Maybe because we're trying to keep the chances of you staying alive higher?"

"We shouldn't be talking about this." I looked away from him. "We're wasting our time and energy when we should be focusing on something more important. Like planning what we should be doing next year."

I wanted to end this discussion and started to turn around. But Arnold grabbed my shoulders and shook them. "Layla! You're not listening! Why do you refuse to listen to us when we're trying our best? When we're trying to–"

"I know! I know..." I grabbed his hands and shook them.

He softened a little. I continued. "But you're more important. Haven't we established this? We have to focus on you."

Arnold took his hands back roughly and was about to say something else when Maria said, "Why risk your life when you could trust a human!"

We both stared at her. She rarely joined in our arguments. She always hated it when we argued. She was our peacemaker. She must have really wanted to change the plan.

I looked them both in the eye and yelled back, "Because humans are never to be trusted! It's because of *her* we are here now. Do we want to repeat history?"

A heavy silence fell in the room. Past events replayed in our minds. I didn't want to bring it up, but I didn't want anyone to forget. Especially the three of us. We needed to work together. Because if we didn't, the whole world would end. I knew without another word that we all agreed on that. Our silence confirmed it.

My phone beeped. That was odd. No one would be messaging me at this time. No. No one would *ever* message me. I had a bad feeling about this. I went into the dining room, picked up my phone and read the message.

Is this your phone? No wonder there was something wrong with it. It didn't have my number. Love Sasha.

I stared and reread the message, again and again. Then I turned to Maria. "I can't believe you gave him my number."

"Sasha has her number?!" Arnold's head snapped and he looked at Maria wide-eyed.

"I thought it would be a good opportunity for you to get to know each other better." She was still upset, but her tone became softer and apologetic.

"He's a human. I don't want to be involved with him. He has his path and I have mine." I looked at my phone again as another message appeared. "I can't believe you gave it to him. Now he thinks we're friends. I'll make it clear to him tomorrow."

I turned around and headed to my room. I didn't want to witness or join in the fight that was about to break out in the kitchen.

He had been trying to act like my best friend all morning. There were multiple text messages already from him. I left them unread. I even ignored the phone calls. I had made a decision. If we met at the bus stop, I would tell him to not talk to me. To never disturb me ever again. There was no reason to continue this exchange and it would stop Maria's planning.

Normally I would ignore him and leave without a single word, but he seemed persistent. I would need to tell him to keep his distance in case he found out my identity again. Then there was Brigid as well. I needed to make myself clear, or else more problems could come out of this. And we'd had enough problems for this year.

"Hey, Layla!"

I turned to see Sasha walking towards me. I was sitting on the bench waiting for the bus at the end of the day. He sat next to me, leaving a space between us.

"I tried calling you. Why didn't you pick up?"

"It's exactly what you think."

"I didn't know I made you that nervous."

I glared at him and he just smiled at me.

"What do you want?" I asked him.

"I just wanted to talk."

"About what?"

"How was your day?" It really was as if we were close enough to have this kind of conversation.

"Sasha, I think there has been a misunderstanding between us." He didn't say anything, so I continued. "I'm grateful for what you've done for me. But other than that, I don't think we should keep in touch with each other anymore."

He sat very still and kept staring at me.

"Is this because I'm Brigid's target?"

"Yes and no."

"I didn't think you were a coward."

"I'm anything but a coward."

"Then I don't see why we can't be friends."

"I don't trust you."

"I guess you haven't forgiven me for what I did."

"You haven't done anything to earn my trust."

"Haven't I?"

For a second I thought his memory had come back, but when I looked at him I realised he honestly believed we were going to be friends. He must have thought that because he took my place as Brigid's target, it had changed my opinion of him. And with the conversation we'd had on the bus and the dinner he'd had with us

150

yesterday, it would look like we'd become friends.

But no, nothing had changed. To me, this whole situation had put me back to where I was always supposed to be. Normal. I wouldn't let that peace be ruined ever again.

"Thank you for helping me. But let's treat each other like we always have. Strangers."

I pulled out my phone and deleted everything he'd sent and blocked his number, right in front of him. He watched me as I did it. Once that was done, I pulled my earphones out, connected them to my phone and plugged them into my ears, ignoring him. Out of the corner of my eye, I could tell he was staring at me in disbelief. He stood up and left without another word.

The bus was late again. The other usual passengers were not here either. I was left alone by myself on the bench. I took out my earphones, disconnected them and slowly wrapped the cable.

We should never have talked to each other on the bus. We should never have had dinner together. We should never have even danced with each other from the start. I put the earphones back in my bag and closed my eyes. How did our lives get so entangled? But it was better this way. No. It should have always been this way.

"Hey! Look who we have here!" I opened my eyes and stared at the voice's owner.

I didn't recognise him. There were two other guys on either side of him. All of them were big, wide and looked untidy, their hands in their pockets. The only familiar thing was our school uniform. They just stared at me with smiles that I knew meant they were up to no good. "Who are you?"

The one on the left smirked. "If we say Brigid's group, would you recognise us then?"

I smiled and stood up very slowly, facing them. I still didn't recognise them, but that didn't matter anymore. If they were from Brigid's group, they could only mean trouble.

This was very bad. I was all alone. There was no one in sight at all. I was surprised that this was happening. I never had any problem travelling from this stop because not a lot of people knew about it. It was supposed to be safe.

I was holding my phone, so there was no way of contacting Arnold without triggering a reaction from them. My options didn't look good at all. If I got hurt, the hail would come and hurt them. If I defended myself, my identity would be revealed. Not to mention if I accidentally hurt them, I would fade away.

Do not panic. I have to stay calm. I can't let it storm. There is always a solution. I just need to think of it.

I looked behind them. No sign of Brigid. That was

a good start.

"What do you want?"

"Nothing much." They took a deliberate step towards me.

I stood my ground.

"You can't do anything to me. I am no longer a target, so you have no right to hurt me."

Keep your emotions in check. Do not feel anything.

"Who says anything about you being a target? We just want some fun."

They took a step closer. Now I took a step back. They had short legs, so maybe I could outrun them back to school where I could call for Arnold and hide out. The school entrance was behind them, so I would have to take the long way around.

"Even Brigid has had enough fun with me, what makes you think you can have the fun? Aren't you worried about facing Brigid's wrath?"

They started laughing and took another step. I took a step closer to the street corner. There was the possibility of an ambush. No one hung around at the back of the school. And even if I yelled for help, no one would come. But I had to try. I had to take that chance.

I can do this.

Suddenly an old white car was honking and speeding towards us. I had prepared to run but now smiled brightly. I never thought I would be so happy to see a human's car.

Arnold parked in the bus lane and jumped out. He ran towards me. The three kids backed up a little bit. They should be afraid.

"Layla, are you okay?" He checked me over. I gave a swift nod.

Then Arnold looked over at the three of them. They backed up even more. When Arnold wanted to be scary, he was terrifying. "If there *was* something wrong, I don't think they would get out alive."

"Let's go." The three of them turned on their heels and ran towards the school.

I shook my head. "You know you can't kill humans."

"Layla, are you sure you're not hurt? Were you afraid? Are you sure you're okay?" he said, shaking my shoulders.

I grabbed Arnold's hands. "Do you see a storm brewing?" He looked up at the sky and then at me. "Do you see any hailstorms happening? I'm completely fine."

"But you were worried, weren't you?" He gave me a look that dared me to lie to his face.

"I'm fine. Let's get in the car."

I sighed with relief as we drove away. Nothing bad happened. There were no weather changes. I wasn't hurt. I was safe. I was okay.

"Thank the heavens I came in time. Or else… or else… or else…" Arnold's grip on the wheel made me afraid it would fall off.

"Nothing would have happened." Then I realised. "Wait, how did you know I was in trouble?"

"Sasha told me."

That made me sit still in my seat. The air-con wasn't on but the temperature in the car went down dramatically. I calmed myself down and got my emotions in check. Now I would have to explain this to the Ministers. Arnold squirmed in his seat.

"What do you mean Sasha told you?"

"Um… So… What happened was, I was maybe ten… twelve minutes away from school when I received a call from Sasha. At first I wasn't going to pick up, but then I realised I had something to say to him, so I did. Before I could say anything, he said that you were in trouble. You have no idea how hard I pressed the brake. I thought the car was going to skid. And then I asked him what he meant by that. And he said he saw a couple of guys from Brigid's gang heading towards the bus stop. So I turned around as fast as I could. And then I yelled at him to save you. And then he said he said he couldn't. And I asked why and he said…"

Arnold glanced at me. I looked out the window into the cloudless sky. "I know what he said. And then?"

"I was quiet for a moment and then I said, if you've become strangers to each other, why are you calling me? And then he said, if you saw an injured person on the road, wouldn't you call for an ambulance? That's why he called me. Even as a stranger, he felt a sense of duty to let someone who could help know that you were in danger. So that's all he had to do. Plus he said he didn't know if Brigid's gang was going to hurt you or not. But he wanted to let me know, just in case... He also didn't want to involve himself, since he was already a target. Then he hung up on me."

I shook my head. That sounded like something Sasha would have said.

"I nearly threw my phone out the window."

"Did Maria give him your number too?"

Arnold was silent for a moment. "No, I asked her for his so that I could text him to let him know not to bother you." More like threatened. That was such an Arnold thing to do. "He helped you again."

"You're the one who saved me."

"Because of *his* help."

I folded my arms, but Arnold continued, "This time if he wanted to, he could have really given up on you. But he didn't. If he did personally save you, then one, he could be targeted even more, and two, well... you didn't want to see him again. So despite all those reasons he still chose to help you. By calling me. Who doesn't like him. And I'm sure he's not fond of me either." Arnold pointed out all the things that I didn't want to admit.

"I never thought there would come a day where you would defend him."

"I'm just thankful for the fact that after the harsh words you threw at him, he still helped you. He could have just let it play out. No one would have known. He must have wanted to let it happen right after you told him you were strangers. Not a lot of people would have done what he did. And you know that."

I didn't say anything for a while. Neither did Arnold. But he knew that I knew. Why did it feel like I was starting to owe him? I looked at Arnold. I couldn't believe he would have a change of heart and come to say something nice about Sasha.

Then again, Arnold and Maria always wanted me to have a human friend. And Sasha happened to be in his good books for now. I still didn't want that plan to happen. It was too risky. And I wasn't willing to either. Especially if it was because of Sasha Reynold. I sighed. Why was this happening?

As if reading my mind, Arnold said, "Maybe he is becoming a better person after all."

CHAPTER FOURTEEN

So much had happened this semester that I was glad it was finally over and the holidays were beginning. I could use the break from school. Before the bell rang, Arnold and I went to our lockers.

Normally Arnold would head off first and go to do his training. But since he thought it was no longer safe to walk alone to the bus stop, he insisted on at least waiting for the bus to arrive, and then he would go.

I convinced him to just drop me off. He was close to driving me back home *and then* going to his training. His training was valuable. I didn't want to take up his time. So we met halfway since it took the least amount of time.

When I got to the bus stop, I prayed that the bus

would come soon and that Sasha wouldn't appear. We'd been avoiding each other since I last spoke to him. He either didn't show up to catch the bus, or I sat on the bus and ignored him when he got on. Today neither wish was granted.

"I didn't know you took the bus," Sasha said to Arnold as he walked towards us.

"I'm only bringing her here."

"Ah… what a great brother. How nice of you." Then Sasha put his earphones in and looked at everything except for us. I was glad he was ignoring us.

Arnold took a deep breath. "Thanks…"

My eyes widened.

"Sorry, what? I didn't hear that." Sasha was now looking at a tree.

"Thanks."

"I forgot! I'm wearing earphones." Sasha took them off and looked at Arnold.

Arnold looked like he'd like to slam Sasha into the tree, but instead he held it in and yelled at him. "Thanks!"

Sasha smiled now.

"If I asked you to run down to the nearest deli and buy one of each kind of food, drink and whatever's there… Would you do it? You know, if you really meant what you said."

I shook my head. Arnold stared at him in disbelief. I thought he was actually going to slam Sasha against that tree when the bus came right on time. Sasha patted Arnold's shoulder. "Just joking. No need to thank me."

Arnold relaxed his shoulders. "Call me if–"

"Sorry, I'm only interested in calling beautiful ladies."

Sasha jumped onto the bus before Arnold could clarify what he meant. I couldn't believe Arnold had thanked Sasha. But I should have known he would, even if he didn't want to. He also didn't like to owe anyone favours.

I waved at Arnold as I stepped on and he waved back. I was about to walk to my usual seat when I saw that Sasha was in the seat in front of it. Since Arnold had thanked him, he was giving me a chance. As if to say that it was my turn.

I would have stopped Arnold if I could. At least he should have thanked him when I wasn't around! Of course Sasha would take this opportunity to make me speak to him. I sat down in my usual seat.

"Don't you have something to say to me?" Sasha prompted when it looked like I wasn't going to say anything to him at all.

"How did you know those guys were coming to the bus stop?"

He was quiet for a bit. He knew he wouldn't be

expecting a thanks just yet. Then he answered. "I was heading back towards the school. When I saw the guys from Brigid's group, I hid. They walked past me and said that they needed to go somewhere where no one would see them, so they mentioned the back of the school. Then I thought of the bus stop. It was along the way and I knew they would see you. And I know what those guys are like. So I called Arnold in case something happened. And I guess something did."

"Why did you help me this time?"

"Because I wanted to."

"Just simply because you wanted to?"

"Yes. Even after how you treated me, I still wanted to."

The bus moved forward with its usual passengers. I was silent as I pondered. Arnold was right. Sasha helped me when he didn't need to. Not right after what I told him. So many things could have happened. Nothing good. Something that Arnold reminded me of in the car constantly. I shouldn't be treating him this way. I hated to admit it, but I did owe him this time. I should thank him properly. I was figuring out how to when he spoke.

"He wasn't the one who should thank me," he muttered, but I heard him clearly. He knew that I needed an opening.

I leaned forward in my seat. "I should give you my thanks."

He leaned towards me. Our faces were separated by the chairs. "Should you?"

"Thank you. After the harsh words I said, you still helped me. So I am thankful for that."

We went back to silence. I had said all I needed to say so I leaned back, folded my arms and closed my eyes. But I could still feel Sasha's gaze on me.

"That's it? That's all I get after I saved you? I'm very disappointed. Maybe a little present would have been nice."

I opened my eyes. He shook his head. I knew this was going to happen. This was what I had been avoiding all along. This was why I was reluctant to thank him. But I knew I couldn't run away from it forever. I would have to face it eventually.

"Dinner?"

"You know what it is."

I did.

"I'm sure Maria would be happy to cook again," I said.

"Your friendship."

Now it was my turn to be quiet for a moment. "That is an enormous and heavy gift to give."

"I'm not asking for much."

"That's not much?"

"Not really."

"Why would you want to be friends with me?"

"Why wouldn't I want to be friends with you?"

"There are a lot of reasons."

"I can think of one really good reason why we should." I waited. "Because we've both been Brigid's victim. We can sympathise with each other."

"I'm sure I'm not the only option."

"You're the best option."

"But don't you hate me? After what I said to you?"

"I was angry. For sure. But I knew I shouldn't just let it happen. Like I said, I know those guys. If they saw you, they would have tried…"

We were quiet for a moment as the rest of his sentence was left unspoken, but we both understood the implications.

"I'm glad that you told Arnold. It was the right choice." It made sense that he didn't come and save me himself. He was Brigid's target, after all. It would have made the situation worse if he'd appeared. "That was very smart of you."

"I'm glad it helped. Now stop trying to change the subject."

"Isn't there anything else you want?"

"Nope."

"Why are you insisting?"

"Why are you hesitating?"

He had absolutely no idea. We kept staring at each

other. So far, his memory of what I am had been erased. Of that I was certain. At least I could be reassured. If I made a bigger deal, things would get more complicated than they already were. And I hated owing people. I absolutely hated it. And that was the only thing he wanted from me. Nothing else. I sighed.

"Fine, we can be friends. But I have a lot of conditions."

"What are they?"

"We can't acknowledge each other at school. We can't hang out in public areas. Keep your distance from me. And you'll never earn my trust. Are you fine with that?"

"That doesn't sound so horrible. That's fine with me."

I couldn't believe he'd accepted those conditions. I didn't think he would. "Are you sure you wanted a friend?"

"I think we'll be really good friends in the future."

He smiled at me and I looked out into the sky and ignored him. Today was even brighter. Where were my rain clouds? I would never have believed I'd agree to have a human friend. What had the world come to?

He pressed the stop button. "You know... you might not mean it, but ever since we've talked, I've felt like I can become the better person I should have been." He stared at me. "You gave me that courage so... thanks..."

The bus stopped and he hopped off without looking back.

* * *

"So you're really, really friends with him now?" Maria asked in excitement.

We were at the dinner table eating our droplet cake. Today the cake tasted like a hailstorm that reminded me of different emotions, like worry, confusion, or disbelief. But I made sure I didn't feel any of those myself. Instead, I focused on my plan. I didn't want to add the Ministers to our problems right now. I leaned my head on one of my hands and with the other poked at the cake. Maria was just beaming. Arnold hadn't said anything during my storytelling.

"I didn't really have a choice."

"Layla, who could ever force you into a decision," Maria teased.

Apparently, Sasha could. But when I thought about it, it was because I felt like I had to pay the debt I owed him. Even if he was asking for the one thing I never wanted to give. I didn't say it out loud but in the end… I felt like I was defeated. Like I'd given in. I hated that feeling. It was frustrating.

"We're technically not friends."

"We know. But it takes time for friendship to grow. Just get to know him."

"I'm not going to make an effort at all."

"Don't worry, Sasha will. You just have to go along with it. You agreed, my dear." Maria knew me well. I always kept my word. "Arnold, what do you think?"

We both looked at him. Arnold was poking at his droplet cake too. "I don't like it." There was hope. "But as much as I dislike him... at least he can protect you too."

I rested my head on the table. All hope was lost. I knew Arnold would be fine with this decision since he was in the same boat as Maria. I sighed. Now I'd be fighting this battle alone.

"Maybe if it was someone else, wouldn't that be better?"

"I think there's no one better," Maria answered.

Arnold sighed and muttered, "I can't believe I'm allowing Sasha of all people to be your friend."

Me neither. I lifted my head. "I'll make him change his mind. He'll stop wanting to be my friend."

"Dear, that's not very nice."

"I gave the conditions. He knows I'm not going to treat him as a friend. He'll give up eventually."

"You never know, maybe we'll be switching plans in the future."

"Maria, can you really see me trusting Sasha?"

The room was filled with silence. She didn't respond. Because she knew me too well. She knew how much I hated humans. Maria clapped her hands, signalling a change of topic. "So how are you guys celebrating your friendship? Lunch at his? Dinner at ours?"

"There is nothing to celebrate!" we both answered.

CHAPTER FIFTEEN

My plan was to ignore him. It was very simple. And that was something I was very good at. He would give up as soon as he realised I wasn't going to put in any effort at all. And who would want to continue being friends with someone who didn't act like one?

For the next two weeks, I ignored all his phone calls and text messages. In fact, I turned off my phone. And in case Sasha dropped by, it was very easy. I would always sneak out with Arnold when he went to his training early in the morning, and I would spend the entire day there with him until I had to meet the Ministers late at night. I heard that Sasha had asked Maria if he could drop by to see me. Maria had tried to convince me to reply, but I never did. I knew she was on his side.

So when we came back from our holiday break, I could tell Sasha was feeling a little awkward and quiet when he walked to the bus stop. We no longer wore our winter uniforms so it was odd to see him in short sleeves. But he should've worn a jumper like me because the first thing that happened to him when he came back was that he saw Brigid. She drew all over his arms with a permanent marker. The images were all gone now, but you could see faint markings on his arm.

"So how was your holiday?"

I ignored him.

"A quiet one, aren't you?"

I ignored him again. He saw I wasn't going to reply so he kept talking. I didn't realise he could talk so much. He talked about his trip up north then he talked about his weekend. Then he switched topics and talked about school, teachers and then students.

It was a side of him I hadn't seen. It was as if I'd met another Arnold. Even when the bus arrived and we sat down, he still wouldn't stop talking. At one point I couldn't handle it anymore.

"Could you please stop talking? I'm getting a headache."

He paused and then asked, "Too much to handle?"

He knew I was purposely ignoring him. But he kept

trying every day. That was alright. I knew it would eventually get to him. And I was right, each day I noticed that he would talk less. Then it became a habit – when I didn't respond he would stop talking and just sit in silence.

Of course it would affect Sasha. It was in his nature. But even then he still continued to make a small effort to start a conversation every day. It didn't seem like he was going to give up.

Because of that, there was a part of me that felt a little guilty. Like I was going back on my word when I agreed to be his friend. But when I thought of the risks and the conditions which he'd agreed on, I continued to act like a stranger.

"You can start the class like this."

It was very unusual for Sasha and Brigid to be here early in the morning. I had just stepped into the hallway, and I witnessed Brigid's group strapping an ice bag onto Sasha's back. Brigid saw me and smiled.

"If you want me to change targets, I can go back to the one before you, if you just say the words."

Sasha didn't even look at me as I turned around and walked out of the hallway. But I could hear him loud and clear. "Or you could just stop having any more victims."

He looked like he was having a hard time. No, he was *definitely* having a hard time. But even then he didn't acknowledge me. Like we were strangers. Like how he agreed to act in front of Brigid. I thought back to all the other conditions I gave him.

He never acknowledged me during school. We never even spent time with each other except on the bus, which no one knew about. And he maintained his distance. He had kept his word. And then there was me, who couldn't make an effort to be his friend. That did make me feel guilty.

After school, when Sasha met me at the bus stop, he looked so happy that it nearly convinced me nothing happened this morning. How could he still have a smile on his face? Arnold saw that I was no longer alone so he said goodbye and left for his training.

"How are you?" Sasha asked me.

I didn't say anything, as usual.

Then I replied, "If I said I'm fine, would you use another pickup line?"

He blinked at me. I'd definitely surprised him. But I had decided. Even if I couldn't be his friend, I should at least respond to him. I did owe him. So the least I could do was talk to him. To hold up my end of the agreement. And then maybe he'd become bored of me and eventually find a new and better friend.

He gave me a charming smile. "Have I already used that one on you?"

"How's your back?"

He became a little stiff. "It's not the worst."

The bus came and we got on. I sat in my usual seat and Sasha sat in front of me.

"I'll be fine," he stated as he turned around in his seat. I raised an eyebrow. Really now? "Because you're looking fine."

He gave me a lazy smile but stared at me intensely. I just made a bored face and turned to look at the sky. With summer, there were hardly ever rain clouds, just puffy white ones. It did make the days seem brighter.

"Oh, come on, please don't give me that reaction."

I didn't respond.

"Are you going to go back to ignoring me again?"

There was an awkward silence on the bus. I kept staring at the sky. But I had told myself that I would talk to him. So I looked at him and responded, "What are you even trying to do?"

"Trying to become better friends."

"Are those the kind of lines for you to make friends?"

"Girls especially. It's a great icebreaker. Works like a charm."

"But I know it's a façade. You don't need to force

yourself to hold that in front of me."

He was completely still, staring at me. Even though I didn't engage in any of the conversations that he started with me, I was still listening. The way he spoke and how he carried the conversation – he would say all the things I liked to hear. He was very skilled. No wonder he was in Brigid's group. But it was no use to me. If I were to have a friend, I would like them to be completely honest with me.

He was silent for a second then he said, "Is that why you haven't spoken to me since we agreed to be friends?"

"It's because of the way you talk. Just say whatever you want to say."

He was silent for another second, deep in thought like this was very new to him. "I see. Okay, then I'll change that. What about jokes? I have some pretty good jokes too."

I leaned back, rested my head on the seat and closed my eyes. Was there any point in me responding?

"What do you call a snowman in the desert?"

I said nothing.

"A puddle."

I couldn't help it. I really tried. I laughed out loud.

* * *

Afterwards, we settled into a new routine. The only

difference from before was that I was responding to him. Sasha still wouldn't speak to me at school and we would ignore each other, but on the bus, he would sit in front of me and would turn around to talk to me.

He would talk about school, his past, and occasionally about Brigid, but most of the time he would make jokes. Some of them were actually funny. Sometimes I would laugh at them, other times I couldn't help but ignore them.

"Today's joke wasn't funny," I told him when I didn't laugh.

"Puddles."

I went into a fit of giggles. I could hardly breathe. My stomach ached so much. I nearly fell off my seat. One of the people at the back made an irritated noise.

But I didn't care. I couldn't stop laughing. Sasha had been surprised the first time he saw me like that. He just kept staring at me with his lips parted. But now he would always bring this joke up.

"I couldn't believe you would laugh at something like that. It wasn't even my best joke. Puddles."

I had been taking deep breaths to calm myself but then started giggling instead. "It's because it melts. So it became a puddle! It's hilarious!"

"You should laugh more often. It makes you look more beautiful."

That made me stop giggling instantly. I looked out into the cloudy sky. It had been a long time since I'd been able to laugh at something as simple as a joke. When was the last time I'd laughed like this? Just the thought made a light drizzle outside.

"Sorry, habits, bad habits. Where do animals go when their tails fall off?"

I didn't say anything.

"Retail store."

I started giggling. Now that one was funny.

He shook his head with a smile on his face. "I can't believe you."

Then for the entire trip, he told all kinds of jokes. Still, nothing dethroned the snowman joke. It was still the funniest.

"Seriously though, you should laugh more often."

"Why do you know so many jokes?"

"I like to read them online."

"Is that the same for your pickup lines?"

"I made those up." He puffed out his chest and held his chin high like he was proud but I raised an eyebrow at him and he deflated. "Okay, I searched them too, but hey they work."

I gave him a nod. "If you say so. Do you like telling jokes more or saying pickup lines more?"

"To tell you the truth, you're the only person I've

told the jokes to."

That didn't surprise me. "I see."

"It just wasn't what a good-looking guy like me was supposed to do. The image people had of me didn't involve me telling jokes. And I had to live up to that expectation. I was surprised when you saw right through me. Well, I'm finally glad I could finally tell my jokes to someone."

That was true. He had the image of that guy who always flirted with a girl. Even I thought of him like that and nothing more. It was a surprise to see this other side of him. Just seeing him telling jokes, it seemed like this was how he normally was. He had been showing me more of his true self than the image he had to play. He seemed happier and more… relaxed?

"By the way," he said. "I might not need to catch this bus anymore. I'm getting my license tomorrow."

"That's good." I'd no longer need to see him all the time.

"I can drop you off home every day after school if you like."

I was just about to say no, but I stopped myself.

It wasn't a bad idea. It would save Arnold the walk to the bus stop every day. And Maria wouldn't need to rush from her workplace to pick me up. I also wouldn't need to worry about Brigid's gang showing up at the bus stop.

It would be so much safer for me if I took his offer. There were many good reasons why I should. But there was one major problem. I would owe him again. It would be like we really were friends.

"No, it's okay. It would be inconvenient for you."

"We're friends. I'm just helping out. What if I asked for your company in the car?"

Since he was offering, and there were more benefits than losses, it really was a good idea. We were acting like friends anyway. "Ask me when you get your license."

* * *

I waited at the bus stop with Arnold as usual.

"Don't go anywhere afterwards."

"Yes, Arnold."

"Go straight home."

"Yes, Arnold."

"Let me know when you arrive home."

"Yes, Arnold."

"Are you sure you want to be in the same car as someone with unproven driving skills?"

"We'll be fine." But I also had my doubts. "And maybe he failed his test, then I won't be able to take the ride." As soon as I mentioned that, a black car stopped right in front of the bus stop. The window rolled down, revealing Sasha as the driver.

"Hey, Arnold. Hop in, Layla."

He rolled up the window and waited for me.

I tried to cheer Arnold up. "It looks fine so far."

That did not reassure him.

He sighed. "This is such a bad idea. Please call me if you think it's not safe. I'll rush back and save you if I need to."

"I know."

Arnold watched as I stepped inside the car, but he didn't move. So I waved and said, "Bye, Arnold."

He walked slowly in the direction towards our white car. I closed the door and put my bag on the floor.

"He worries too much," Sasha said, watching Arnold, who kept turning his head back towards us.

"He has reason to."

"But welcome to Sasha's Services." I ignored him as I put my seatbelt on. "Are you ready?"

Arnold was right. This was a bad idea. What if I got into a car accident? I didn't even know if he was a good driver. Taking the bus was safer than being in a car with Sasha Reynold. I tightened my grip on my seatbelt. "Now I want to change my mind."

"You're safe with me."

I highly doubted that and he knew. "Seriously, everything is going to be just fine."

He changed gear and began to reverse, then abruptly halted. I was so shocked that I took my seat belt off and held onto the door handle. I was about to rip the door open when Sasha started laughing.

All of a sudden, the temperature was so cold that I could even see my own breath. Oh no. Not right now. In a matter of seconds, I covered his eyes with one hand and with the other I turned on the heater full blast.

Sasha was laughing so hard he couldn't have noticed how cold it was. He covered my hand with his. But I kept it on his eyes. I'd never held onto something so tightly. Thank the winter ancestors he was weak from all the laughing, so he didn't make an effort to take my hand away. And I mentally thanked Maria, who'd taught me the car button functions. Who would ever have thought I'd need to know? And I'd been so reluctant to learn them from Maria.

"I'm embarrassed. Don't you dare look at me," I said in my high girly voice, but I was giving him the death stare.

"That... was so... funny..."

As much as I wanted to leave him dead cold, I couldn't afford for him to find out my secret again. I directed all the fans onto him while I took deep, silent breaths. I focused on calming my nerves. Meanwhile, he continued to laugh.

Please let the temperature turn back to normal soon. Please let it be back to normal now.

Slowly, very slowly, the air turned warmer. I sighed internally. Thank the winter ancestors. I turned off the heater, redirected the fans and took my hand off his eyes. That was close. So, so close. I thought the cold would last longer than that, but it left quicker than I would have imagined.

"I'm sorry. I won't do it again." He was rubbing his jaw and smiling. I just glared at him. "Did you turn on the air conditioner?"

"Yeah, because I thought you needed to cool your head."

Sasha looked suspicious, but I was still giving him a glare. I didn't think he could figure out what happened anyway. He didn't see anything. He must have felt the cold for a few seconds, not enough to reach a conclusion. He shrugged it off.

"I'm sorry, I couldn't help it." He was smiling again. I gave him a sweet smile.

"You can let go of my hand now." He glanced down at my hand grasped in his and let it go. I took my hand away.

"You touched me first."

"Because I didn't want you to see me embarrassed."

"Now I wish I got to see it."

Finally, he got the car on the road. I thought we'd

have an accident any second, but the longer he drove, the safer I felt. I couldn't believe he tried to scare me as a joke. He started making conversation, but I ignored him.

"Are you angry with me?"

I still didn't reply.

"It was just a joke."

"I didn't find it funny." My tone made him freeze. Then he softened his tone.

"Okay, I'm sorry. I won't do it again. Please forgive me."

I went quiet again.

"Please forgive me. I'll owe you a favour."

I was about to say the favour when he continued, "As long as we're friends."

He knew what I was thinking. Fine, I'd accept that at least.

"Are we okay now?"

"Fine," I replied.

He smiled at that, but then his face went serious again. "Can I ask something?"

"That depends."

"Your condition… How did you find out?"

That was sudden. It was something I hadn't expected him to ask. Especially right after what just happened. Of course I couldn't tell him the truth, but I'd always had the same answer to that question since the teachers asked.

"I actually don't know how it happened. All I know is that ever since I can remember, I've been afraid of water. I couldn't be near it or else I knew that I wouldn't be safe."

"What did… it feel like?"

I'd never been asked that question. Although I was not really afraid of water, I described to him something similar.

"Like you've been trapped in a cage and it's thrown underwater. You're drowning and there's no escape. It's suffocating and frightening and it's like you can never escape, but you know you have to endure as long as possible or else that's the end."

We were silent for a while, then Sasha said, "Is there a cure?"

I just had to wait for my coming of age and this would stop. "My psychologist said that it'll come with time. I think that might be true."

He raised an eyebrow. "That simple?"

"I would hope so."

We stopped at a red light. He looked at me and rolled his side of the window down. "I hope so too, cause you're missing out on life."

I gave him a small smile. "What would I be missing out on?"

"A lot of things." He started to list them with one

hand, keeping the other hand on the wheel. "Good food. Good places. Good people. And especially, great experiences. You haven't tried the desserts in Northbridge or seen the circus and its tricks or even played at the Royal Show. It would be sad if you never tried them before you die."

"Sounds like a must."

"Of course. It's the smallest joy as well as the happiest moments that make life beautiful." He threw a smile at me. "And when you finally get over your fear, I'll take you to the beach. And I'll teach you how to surf so you'll know how cool the water is. It'll be fun."

Suddenly, a girl in the passenger seat of the car next to us yelled, "Hey!"

We both turned to look at her. She was blonde and beautiful and was only looking at Sasha. "I just wanted to say that you're really hot!"

I watched as Sasha propped his arm on the door and gave her a dashing smile. I rolled my eyes. Her friend in the driver's seat was smiling and watching the whole exchange.

"You know, you might be asked to drive soon," Sasha replied. "You're making the other women look really bad."

She giggled, then turned from the window, grabbed a piece of paper and wrote on it. She scrunched it up and threw it through Sasha's window.

"Call me if you want company!" she shouted. He gave her a wink as a reply and then the light turned green so we drove off.

Sasha continued happily rambling on about other things that we could do as if this happened every day. But I wasn't really listening. I'd forgotten that he was popular with the girls. I looked at Sasha. He looked like he enjoyed it. And that he was used to girls throwing themselves at him. He also couldn't help himself from charming girls, could he?

That must have been why he would always use pickup lines. I guessed it was a habit he'd formed. It made sense why he would occasionally say those lines to me, even when I'd told him not to.

Then I really looked at him.

For the first time, I could see that he was good-looking. With his structured face and warm brown eyes, no wonder so many girls had fallen for him. How was it that he was in front of me now and treating me as a friend when he could have chosen anyone else?

I spoke my thoughts out loud. "I'd forgotten how popular you once were."

He stopped mid-sentence, but then replied with confidence, "I am a feast to the eyes."

I rolled my eyes. My brief appreciation of him was

gone. "I guess you are."

"Then who would you consider handsome?"

"I don't know. I don't care about those things."

He thought about it for a moment and nodded. "Who would you pick? Me or Arnold?"

"Arnold."

"I mean in terms of looks."

"Still Arnold."

"Now you're just being biased."

"If good looks were your only redeeming quality, then you're as good as a black cat."

"No way are you serious."

"Keep your eyes on the road!"

"Are you saying that I cause other people's deaths?"

"You've given me nothing but trouble."

"I should at least be a charming fox."

"You're lucky I didn't classify you as an arthropod."

By the time we reached my house, he still hadn't been elevated from his position as a black cat. When we got out of the car, Maria was already at the door.

"Layla! You made it back alive!"

Sasha shook his head. "Maria, I'm hurt. You should give me more credit."

"In celebration, why don't you stay for dinner with us?"

I gave Maria a look. Why does she always insist on

dinner? I already knew what Sasha would say.

"I'd love to. But please cook less."

Maria went into the kitchen and Sasha and I headed into the dining area and made a start on our homework. Once again, Sasha teased me when he saw that I was stuck on a question. I didn't want him to tease me anymore about it, so I told him the truth. That Arnold did give me answers.

"That's cheating. Aren't you worried about your grades?"

"It's only one class. I do well in all the others."

"But you never know. What if you need this class to get a better university entrance exam result?"

"I'm not going to take it."

Sasha widened his eyes. "Why?"

"Because I don't want to."

"Don't you have a goal for the future?"

"What about you? What are your plans?"

"Don't know. But I want to keep my grades up just in case I need them to get into a good university. You should do it too."

I shrugged and turned back to the homework.

"We could get into the same university," Sasha suggested.

"Because I don't have enough of your presence already."

"It'll never be enough."

I rolled my eyes. The front door opened. Arnold looked into the dining room and sat down next to me.

"You can just copy mine. It's fine for you not to do it."

I looked triumphantly at Sasha. Sasha looked at Arnold.

"Help me convince her to take university entrance exams."

That brought an awkward silence in the room. Sasha looked confused. He didn't know what was wrong. Arnold was about to argue back when Maria called from the kitchen. Arnold took the cue and went into the kitchen.

"Did I say something wrong?"

"Nothing. You're just annoying," I said and Sasha winked at me.

"Did you forget that they're supposed to be bonding? You're interrupting them," Maria whispered, but we heard her anyway. Sasha just smiled.

"Your mum likes me."

"But Arnold doesn't like you."

"I'll have to work my way into his good books."

"Good luck with that."

Sasha and I continued our studies while Arnold and Maria cooked. When Maria finished, we set the table and helped her bring out the food. There was definitely less food than last time. But there were some dishes that I'd never seen.

Sasha looked nervous. "Are most of these for me again?"

"Of course they are!" Maria said. "I hope you enjoy them."

I smiled and took a small portion of everything. Sasha took a chicken leg from one of the plates and gave it to me.

"It's the best part. You should have it."

"Thanks, but you should have it." I gave the piece back to him instead and he smiled.

Maria and Arnold exchanged a look that I didn't like. Sasha managed to finish every dish that was there. We started clearing the table. Arnold and Maria headed towards the kitchen while Sasha and I stacked the plates.

"You guys go watch TV or something, we'll manage out here," Maria said, pushing Sasha towards me.

"No, it's fine. I should head home. It's pretty late already," Sasha said after looking at Arnold's face.

"If you insist... Dearest Layla, could you please walk him to the door?"

Sasha went to get his school bag while Maria and Arnold continued to clean up. I felt bad for not helping them. As if Maria was able to read my mind, she nodded her head towards Sasha. I gave her a face and followed him to the door.

"By the way, here are the spare keys." He put them on top of the cupboard in the hallway.

"Spare keys for what?"

"To my car. If you're going to ride with me from now on, you should at least wait inside it instead of standing around. It'll be safer that way."

I was speechless. I didn't think he'd have thought that far ahead. "Thanks... I really appreciate it."

Sasha smiled. "No problem."

He opened the door and stepped out. "I'll be parking near the bus stop. So you can wait in the car until I come out of classes." He paused for a moment. "And I'm sorry for scaring you today."

"This is why you're giving me free rides from school."

"I could make it up to you with something else."

"Like what?"

A silence fell between us while I waited for his answer. But he just kept staring at me, like he wanted to do something. He shook his head.

"I'll wait until you're comfortable, but for now sweet dreams."

I raised an eyebrow at him, but he turned and went to his car. He waved at me and drove away. I went back inside and grabbed the keys Sasha had left for me. It felt strange as if I owned the car as well. Even Arnold hadn't given me his spare car keys. I walked back into the kitchen, where Arnold and Maria were finishing up the dishes.

"What's that you're holding?" Maria asked.

"Sasha's car keys." The water stopped running as Maria and Arnold stared at me. "His spare ones. It wasn't my idea."

"It looks like you guys are closer than we thought," Arnold said.

"We are not that close."

"But you look like you at least get along with each other."

"I don't hate him as much as I used to if you think that's an improvement."

"Yes, it is. It definitely is." Maria smiled and elbowed Arnold. I knew what she was implying.

"I still don't trust him with my life."

"I know dearest, I know."

"Is it just me?" We both looked at Arnold as he spoke. "But does it seem like he likes you?"

The room became silent again. Then I started to laugh. "Sasha? Liking me?" But Maria gasped and touched Arnold's shoulder. That made me stop laughing.

"You could see it too?" Maria said.

I kept looking between them. I couldn't believe it

would ever cross their minds that Sasha would like me.

"He does not," I stated.

"Dear, he's liked you for a while now. I'm surprised that Arnold caught on."

I shook my head. "There is no way."

"How do you know?"

"He flirted with a girl right in front of me today. If he liked me, he wouldn't have done that, right?"

"Maybe he was trying to make you jealous?"

"Remember what Arnold told me? He likes to charm girls." Arnold nodded at my statement.

"It won't be so bad if he likes you, dear."

Arnold and I looked at Maria.

"Why would we want that?" I said at the same time as Arnold said, "That's a bad idea."

"I don't see any problems."

Arnold and I exchanged a look. We could see so many problems with that.

"If we kissed, the entire Winterland would know."

"I didn't ask you to kiss him. I'm just saying that it would be easier for him to cooperate with us if he liked you. That way you can trust him."

"That's never going to happen."

"I don't know, dear. It looks like you've grown closer to him."

"That's true, but only because I'm acting as a friend."

"Acting as a friend or have you really become friends with him?"

I was quiet but then said, "Acting as a friend."

"Hmmmm, I don't think so." Maria smiled.

"I am. End of discussion."

I no longer wanted to argue with Maria and I didn't want to acknowledge anything more than what we were saying right now because I knew for a fact that there was nothing between us.

CHAPTER SIXTEEN

For the next couple of days, I waited for Sasha after classes in his car so that he could drop me home. There were days when Maria wasn't yet home, so we agreed we'd be in a nearby library. I did not want to be home alone with Sasha. Other times Sasha wanted to drive somewhere else, but every time I would remind him I wasn't allowed to.

I was being very careful around him. I didn't want to risk him finding out anything suspicious again. But it was easy to hide it from him when he was careful and protecting me from my "fear" as well. For a moment, I even thought it might be possible to be friends with a human, as long as they knew where I stood. But that thought disappeared every time Sasha dropped a pickup line.

I was also trying to keep my distance from him. I didn't want to give Maria any more hope than she already had. Plus, I wanted to avoid any emotional attachments that might form between us. That was why sometimes he would stay for dinner, but other times he would leave right after dropping me off.

Arnold was also slowly getting used to having Sasha around, except there were times when he still kicked him out. Like when Sasha stayed for dinner today and Arnold was upset with his jokes.

I was ready to tell him he should leave for the night when he said, "Let's watch a movie afterwards."

"We don't have any movies at home," Arnold stated.

"I brought my DVDs." Sasha pulled out a case from his bag.

"We don't have a DVD player."

"I thought Maria had one." Sasha looked confused.

We turned our heads to Maria. She smiled sheepishly. "I just brought one recently thinking it'd be nice if we could watch movies together."

Arnold and I were too surprised to say anything.

"Arnold, you can help me wash the dishes. You two enjoy the movie."

"But I want to-" Arnold started, but he was dragged

by Maria to the kitchen. My shoulders slumped. I was left alone with Sasha again.

"Can we watch in your room?"

"Could you leave for the day?"

"One movie. And I will leave for the night," Sasha countered.

"No. It's already late, you should leave."

"I ate so much. I can't drive like this. It wouldn't be safe."

We could argue all night and it would get us nowhere. I could no longer be bothered and it was only a movie so I sat on the couch. Sasha turned off the lights, turned on the television and grabbed a disc. I flipped through his collection while he set everything up. It was my first time seeing them so I hadn't known there were so many movies to choose from. He came to sit next to me and when I looked at the screen the first thing I saw was human blood.

I covered my eyes and turned towards Sasha.

"Is this horror?!" I asked in surprise.

"Didn't you see the DVD menu?"

I sneaked a peek and there was more blood. I closed my eyes.

"We can watch another one." I looked at Sasha. He seemed a little worried. Then he changed his tone to teasing. "I never knew you'd be afraid of horror."

I didn't want to lose. Not after I had allowed him to choose the movie. "We can continue with this one."

It was just a movie. It wasn't like I made it happen. But I was still nervous. So much human blood. If I ever caused that to happen to any human... even just a scratch... So I decided to lie down, pretending to watch the movie, but in reality I was closing my eyes. I needed to calm my nerves.

I didn't cause that. It's just a fictional story. I'm alright. I am okay. I am not afraid.

The sound of the movie stopped. I opened my eyes and the screen was blank. I sat up and looked at Sasha.

"There's no point if you're not watching. How about we dance?" He extended his hand to me. I looked at it. Then he surprised me again. "You looked so scared."

"How did you know dancing calms me down?"

"I know how you enjoy dancing. I could tell when we were partners in the dance lessons." I didn't think he'd have noticed such a thing. "I thought it would make you feel better."

"But we don't have any music."

It was as if I gave him permission because he got his phone out and played a ballroom kind of song. He stood up and grabbed my hands, pulling me up. Before I could resist, he grabbed me by the waist and brought our bodies close to each other.

I was going to push him away, but he took my hand and placed it on his shoulder. He grabbed my other hand and started to move. He led the dance and I couldn't help but follow.

The song kept playing and we moved around the room avoiding all the furniture. Arnold and Maria were still in the kitchen. If they were talking, I couldn't hear a thing. At first, I was a little uncomfortable but I relaxed pretty fast when he gave me a twirl. Even though I didn't want to admit it, I was already feeling better.

"I'm sorry. I didn't know that the movie would scare you so much. I didn't think the brave Layla would be afraid of anything."

"I wasn't scared." He raised an eyebrow at me. I looked away. "At least you stopped the movie. And offered to dance."

"What do you call a fake noodle?" he asked.

I shook my head.

"An impasta."

I smiled.

"What do you call an apology written in dots and dashes?"

I shook my head again.

"Re-morse code."

I giggled. That was a funny joke.

"Puddles."

I couldn't help it. I started laughing.

"That was the sound I wanted to hear."

He smiled at me as I smiled back at him. The next song played on his phone. It was a slow song, and so he pulled me into an embrace and we just swayed to the music. I wrapped my arms around his neck and the last of the giggles left me.

It was nice to laugh like this. I would never have thought that it would be, with Sasha. Especially when he was suffering in his own way too. Every day he was still suffering from Brigid's bullying antics. I couldn't imagine how much damage and trauma had built up within him. He didn't show it, but I knew it affected him. And yet, he chose to be here, to make jokes and laugh with me.

"Are you going to stay as Brigid's target forever?"

"I'm being punished right now."

"There are other ways to redeem yourself."

"Do I have a choice?"

"You could fight back."

"Do you know how many people are in her gang?"

"That doesn't matter. You can always choose to fight back. Instead of just punishing yourself, why not punish the person who doesn't see their own fault?"

Sasha didn't reply, but I could tell he was thinking.

"I know you are smart enough to pull it off. Plus,

you were her second in command, you know the secrets. You're the perfect person to bring her down."

"Would you help?" he asked. He said it casually, but I knew he was hoping for a yes.

"No. You know I wouldn't put myself in a situation like that."

Sasha tried not to show his disappointment. "I was hoping for a different answer."

"I'll give you my honest opinion on your plans."

"I'll think about it."

"I'm just thinking that it would be fair for everyone to be punished. Not just you."

We didn't say anything for a while. He just stared at me and I looked at him curiously. Then I realised how odd this situation was. No matter how many times we hung out, I would never have thought that I'd be here, dancing in the dark in the middle of my living room with Sasha Reynold. If anyone had told me this would happen, I'd never have believed it.

I guess we had become close to one another. And I guess I could even call him a friend, as much as I didn't want to admit it, and not that I was going to tell him either. I did enjoy his jokes. And I did enjoy the distraction. No, I didn't trust him completely but I was a bit thankful for these moments. And it was because of him.

"Thanks."

He was so surprised that he froze for a few moments. "For what?"

"For the jokes. And for the dance. I know you're having a hard time, but you still tried to cheer me up. I just wanted to say thank you."

He was quiet for a moment. "I didn't think you would say these kinds of things."

I shrugged. "When I need to say something, I do."

Sasha nodded slowly. I noticed a slight change in him. His eyes kept straying to his phone, then to me and then back to his phone. He bit his bottom lip. He looked like he wanted to say something.

In all the time since I'd met Sasha, I had never seen him so nervous. He was always so confident that I thought there could never be anything that would make him this way. It was quite funny watching this. Then in the softest tone,

"Do you… do you want to go to the ball with me?"

The room was filled with the song that came from his phone. He stared at his phone, but I kept looking at him. I was waiting for his eyes to come back to me, but they didn't. Seeing him staring at his phone without giving me a glance made his words even more genuine than I thought. Because even I knew the hidden meaning when a boy asks a girl out to the ball.

I nearly stopped swaying, but I kept moving or else

it would have become too awkward. I wanted to doubt my hearing. But then he finally looked at me. His warm brown eyes never wavered as they bored into mine. And that was when I realised it was real. He was being very sincere.

Sasha kept dancing with the confidence he once had. My body automatically moved as he led me around the room, lost in my own thoughts. I wasn't expecting any of this. Was this a confession of his feelings? He couldn't *really* like me. It didn't make any sense. When would he have started to like me? Why would he?

He was waiting for a reply, but I didn't know what to say to him.

The second song ended and there was no third. The room was silent. We stopped moving. I removed my arms from his neck, but he didn't move his from my waist. He stared at me. He searched my face and held my gaze. Then he tightened his hold on me, bringing my face closer to him. I held my breath. His eyes trail down to my lips. For a moment I thought he was going to kiss me, but then suddenly he let go of me.

"It's quite late. I should probably head home."

I let out the air I was holding. "Good idea."

He took his bag and headed towards the door. I walked with him. He turned back to me as if he wanted to say something. But then settled with, "Sweet dreams."

I nodded. He walked to his car and got in, then rolled down the window and waved at me. I just stared at him and he pulled away down the driveway. When he was out of sight, I heard Maria and Arnold exit the kitchen. I closed the front door and headed towards them. Maria held a droplet cake out to me. I took it and sat on the couch.

"I can't believe what just happened," I started.

"I can't believe what I heard!" Arnold sat on the other couch and dug into his own droplet cake.

"Why, what's wrong?" Maria asked curiously. "I thought it was sweet of him to ask you to the ball even though you're going with Arnold."

I didn't want to answer so Arnold explained instead. "Maria, you don't know this but if a guy asks a girl to the ball, it basically means they're confessing their feelings. That they like the other party."

Maria gasped. I'd been overhearing all the girls in our class talking about their ball dates. How the boys asked them. How some of them were more than friends now.

"So he just confessed?!"

"Not exactly. He would have asked to go just as friends." I wanted to believe this. "You've seen people asked to the ball as friends."

Arnold gave me a sceptical look. "We both know it's more likely that they have feelings for the other. And

Sasha didn't even say he wanted to go as friends."

"That can't be."

"Why Layla, it was pretty obvious." Maria shrugged as she sat opposite me. I sat very still. I could feel that Arnold had stopped fuming and was sitting very still.

Then I sat up straight. "That's just ridiculous. Are we going with this theory again?"

But I could see what they were trying to say because my mind began a quick flashback. When Sasha had first blocked that water bottle. When Sasha called Arnold to help me. Every time Sasha flirted with me. The car rides. Tonight.

I shook my head. "Sasha Reynold? Likes me? Have we lost our minds?"

"Sweetheart, why else would he help you to this extent? Let's say that it's because he feels guilty for what he's done to you. He would have repaid that when he first helped you. And do you know how many times he has helped you now? Then let's say that it's because you are friends. We all know how deep your friendship runs. It's not deep enough. Is putting his life at risk worth it? If you're worth it, it's only because of one reason. He loves you, my dear."

"He didn't risk his life."

"Okay, I was exaggerating, but it still doesn't change the fact that he's done a lot for you."

Maria had made me speechless. I couldn't think of any way to counter-argue. She was right on every point. But every single human cell in my body refused to believe what she said. There had to be another reason. It couldn't be as simple as him *liking* me. This was Sasha Reynold. He could get any girl he wanted. Except for me, but he would eventually forget and give up on me. He could get better girls and he knew that. Why me? *If* he liked me, that was.

"The most important question is, how do you feel?" Arnold asked.

Maria and Arnold looked at me.

I raised my eyebrows.

"Do you think I would fall for him?"

"Sasha is quite good-looking, dear. And he's got a pretty good personality now too. You two would look good together."

"Mum!" Arnold exclaimed.

"You know how I feel," I answered, and Arnold sighed in relief. "I'm not going to make a mistake."

"But if he's been with you for a while now, don't you feel anything for him at all?" Maria asked.

"I'm starting to think that you would like me to."

Maria stopped smiling. "No, we wouldn't want that."

I sighed. "This is a problem."

"I still don't see how this is a problem." Maria shrugged.

"*If* he likes me, he will try to make me like him."

"Which you won't."

"No, I won't. But it won't stop him from making advances."

"It can't be that bad."

"He tried to kiss me just now." Maria and Arnold blinked at me. "The Ministers would have found out the moment his lips touched mine. Can you imagine what would have happened? Maybe I should stop being friends with him?"

Maria and Arnold looked at each other and held hands. I ignored them and ate my cake. They were having a private conversation without me. But I had an idea.

If he wanted to be more than friends, then there was only one answer I could give. And I wasn't worried because it was an easy solution. I would need to make it clear to Sasha in case something like this happened again. I wouldn't want any surprise advances from him. But I was confident he didn't like me. Why would he when I had done nothing to make him?

"We know how you feel towards humans," Maria said. "So there would be no way you would fall for Sasha. We just want you guys to be friends. Nothing more than that. I think it's safe to say you guys could stay as friends. You just need to be clear with Sasha about that." He was their only hope for *their* plan. They wouldn't want to lose that.

I nodded, "Alright, I'll ask him clearly what he means tomorrow then."

"Don't hurt his feelings, dear," said Maria.

CHAPTER SEVENTEEN

"Arnold, is it just my imagination or do you think you've improved? I think you can do nearly three-quarters of the list now."

We were driving back home from another night of winter making. The morning light shone down on us. Something about it made me believe today was going to be a good day.

"I think so too."

I looked at him excitedly. "That's good news Arnold! Maria would be so excited to hear about it. We have to continue what we're doing so we could be better. Do you know what changed?"

I was so proud of Arnold. This was the most progress

we've had in a while and in the shortest amount of time as well. Maybe we could succeed with our plan.

"I don't know but something does feel different."

"Maybe it's because you're nearly of age."

Arnold nodded slowly. "Maybe. But also recently, everyone feels a little bit... happier? So I don't know but I feel less nervous and more calmer when I'm making winter."

I sat still. I knew what he was thinking. What he was trying to refer to. One of the reasons why we were relaxed recently was because one person entered our lives. Arnold continued, "Maybe having Sasha around was not too bad right?"

"Don't worry Arnold. I'm just making things clear with him. I won't go back on my word. I'll still be friends with him."

So I waited after school in the usual spot where Sasha parked the car. I knew what to do. But I didn't know how to bring up the topic. No one had ever made advances on me. I should've asked Maria when I had the chance. But she would be an unreliable source of information since she was biased towards Sasha. I was still trying to think of a plan when Sasha rounded the corner and headed towards me.

"Why didn't you wait inside the car?"

"There's something wrong with the car key."

I showed him. I pressed the button and then pulled on the door handle, but it wouldn't open.

"Let me try."

I handed him the keys. He tried exactly what I did but it wouldn't open for him either. "I think it ran out of battery. I'll change it when we get back to your place."

I nodded and waited for Sasha to let us into the car. But nothing happened. Then I looked at him and he was still standing right in front of me. I gave him a questioning look.

"So what's your answer?" he asked.

"My answer?" I didn't think I had to give an answer.

He pushed a strand of hair away from my face. I moved away. "Do you want me to ask again?"

Now I felt like he was hinting at a new question. Before I could say anything he continued, "Layla... I- Layla!"

Everything happened so fast. He pulled me towards him as someone behind me grabbed my bag from my arm. Sasha kept me behind him with my back on the car. I looked over his shoulder and couldn't believe who I saw.

"Surprise!" Brigid waved at us. "We saw you so we wanted to say hi."

Why hadn't we seen her? She was with her gang; how was it possible we missed them? They must have seen us a while ago... since I've been here. They must have waited in their cars. I looked around us. There were other parked cars. They must have belonged to Brigid's gang. How could this coincidence have happened? I never thought we would meet anyone while we were out.

"I didn't expect to see you guys together."

The guy who took my bag opened it and started looking inside. At first I was afraid when I saw Brigid, but when I thought about it, this wasn't the worst. There were only five other boys. No audience. There were no weapons in their hands. And they didn't look angry, so they could only want some fun. The guy took my phone and showed it to Brigid. She nodded and he put it back in the bag and zipped it up.

"Don't worry. Let's get out of this together," Sasha whispered to me.

"Alright," I whispered back.

We could do this. We just needed to give her what she wanted and then she'd leave us alone.

"I think we have a lot to talk about," she said. "After all this time, it seems like we didn't have a chance to clear things up or have a proper talk." That was because she was relentlessly punishing him. "But now I'm ready to listen, so let's have a chat."

"Okay then, let's talk this out," Sasha said casually.

"Why did you betray me?"

"You know why."

Brigid didn't like his answer. Suddenly, she stepped back and two of the guys rushed forward, grabbed Sasha and pulled him to the side, leaving me by the car by myself. They started searching his body. They found his phone and his car keys and kept them.

"Was it for her?" Brigid looked at Sasha and pointed at me.

"No…"

"You like her, don't you?"

There was silence. I looked at Sasha and he was looking at me. I didn't want to interpret his expression. Why didn't he answer no?

Brigid turned to look at me. The other guy pulled something out. A water bottle. I stood very still. Brigid held the water bottle and examined it. That was if there was water in it. I looked away and pressed myself to the car as much as I could. I acted as if I was terrified. But inside, I was very calm. I had to be in control of my emotions. I should have pretended to faint. But that would make me more vulnerable than I already was. She could do anything to me if I fainted.

"Are you guys dating?"

No one said a word.

"Maybe I should make myself clear." Brigid nodded at the boys.

The first blow was a punch to his stomach. The second was an elbow in his back that brought him down to the floor. I didn't react. I couldn't react. I wanted to say something but knew it wouldn't help him. It would confirm her suspicions. And it would make her angrier than she already was. And who knew what else she would do. I focused on calming my nerves.

We'll be okay. It'll be alright. I have to be calm and think through our options.

Whatever we did could either save us or break us.

"What's your relationship with him?" Brigid directed the question at me.

"Nothing."

"Then why are you two together?"

"We just spoke a few words. I was going to leave."

"It didn't seem like that to me."

Sasha was on the ground, gasping for air. The boys picked him up. I wanted to do something. I wanted us safe. But that was impossible. The situation changed as soon as we were separated and a water bottle appeared.

As hard as I tried to think of a plan to save us both, there was none. There was no way for us to go unscathed. He knew that as much as I did. No phones. No car. No one else in sight. Five against two. I knew he realised the situation we were in. There was nothing that we could do.

Except I could use my powers.

That was a very dangerous line of thought. There were so many things that could go wrong. Everything I had planned would be destroyed. Revealing my magic. My death. A human death. That was a very big risk. As much as I hated humans, I did not want to kill them.

I was contemplating what action to take when Brigid started talking. "Let's do something fun. I will give you two choices. You can either stay with me or you may leave."

That was too simple. She had something more planned. We waited for her to finish.

"Both may stay. But only one can leave."

In other words… one of us had to get hurt.

"If you two choose to leave, then we play a game to see who gets to leave." She then smiled.

Brigid was so cruel. She was playing with us. If there was a chance we could both escape, then of course we'd take it. As a ruler, I still had many things I needed to do. I had to protect my plan. At any cost. Sasha was human. He wouldn't want to get hurt either. If he could use me to get out of his situation, then he would. Because that was in his nature.

"So what is your choice? Who wants to stay? Who wants to go?"

Neither of us answered.

"I guess we haven't learnt our lesson yet."

Brigid passed the water bottle to one of the boys and he opened it. This was very bad.

"Right now, the person you want to hurt the most is me. Let her go and you can deal with me."

Brigid and I turned to look at Sasha.

Sasha, who spoke those words. Sasha, who had made his choice. Sasha, who chose to stay. He looked worried and scared for me. But he also looked determined. Determined to keep me safe. Even in this state. In this situation. I couldn't believe he would do that for me.

Everyone was silent. Then Brigid started laughing.

"You really do like her. Wow... I can't believe this. You betrayed me because of a girl. Because of this girl."

Brigid nodded at the boys near Sasha and they punched him in the stomach again.

Could I really leave Sasha here alone with Brigid? Right after he chose to make himself bait? But if I stayed...

Sasha was coughing. I didn't make a sound, but it hurt to see him like this. He didn't deserve it. Did I want him to suffer more for me? Sasha fell to the floor again and the boys started kicking him.

"And what is your choice? I've changed my mind. If you choose to stay with me, I'll let him go."

I hesitated. I'd known what my choice was from the very beginning. If I could use any human to save myself,

I would never hesitate.

I would sacrifice them.

But this time was different. Even when he could have saved himself, he chose to help me instead. Didn't I owe him that? Shouldn't I return the favour? Should I take his place? But I had my powers. Should I risk it? Should I use them? As a friend, I should stay. As a ruler, I should leave. His eyes met mine – begging for mercy. I knew what I had to do.

"You can hurt him. And let me go."

I hated this. Every single word I just spoke. But I had no other option. Yes, I could use my powers. But would I risk everything when Brigid gave me the option to simply leave? By sacrificing Sasha?

I met Sasha's stare.

I was willing to sacrifice him.

Sasha looked devastated. I felt like I'd thrown him away. Like how you dump your trash. As if he was nothing. He looked hurt. I looked away. But I knew that he was putting on a show to convince Brigid. He had to.

At first, Brigid froze and just stared at me, but then she threw her head back and laughed. "See. Did you see that, Sasha? The girl that you like only cares about herself. She just used you. Bring a car," she said to one of the boys.

I glanced back and really looked at Sasha. No, he

was hurt. Sasha looked away from me. His eyes told me how disappointed he was. My heart felt heavy. It felt like I'd made the wrong choice.

One of the guys by Brigid's side crossed the road and left. What was she thinking now?

"While we wait for the car, let's have some fun," Brigid said. "Break a rib."

No...

The other four guys grabbed Sasha and started kicking him in the ribcage. Sasha didn't call for help. He didn't yell or scream. He took a lot of sharp breaths.

I wanted to tell them to stop. I wanted to sweep them away with my wind. I wanted to do something for him. But all I could do was watch. I couldn't help him. I couldn't risk it. I didn't move. I don't think I was breathing. I couldn't think of anything. I couldn't bear to watch this any longer.

I tore my eyes away from him. But when I did, I heard a finger snap. That was when I heard Sasha scream. I looked back at them. She had ordered one of the boys to step on his hand hard enough that it drew blood.

I leaned against the car. Human blood. My heart ached. This time I really couldn't breathe. It didn't matter that Brigid was watching me. I clutched my chest. This wasn't my fault. I didn't do this. I didn't hurt him. But the sight of blood made me dizzy. It made me feel weak – it felt like a storm was brewing.

No, I can't let that happen.

I stood up straight and turned away from Brigid. I closed my eyes and took quick breaths. I could still hear the kicks. I could hear Sasha gasping for air, even his occasional screams. I could hear my own heart beating fast. But I controlled my emotions. I tried not to think of what I'd just seen. I tried to clear my thoughts. I tried to ignore everything around me. *I'm sorry, Sasha.*

Finally I heard the car. I opened my eyes.

"One of you can take her to the car."

The guy with my bag walked up to me. Without a word, I snatched it off him and started towards the car. I had to get out of there. I had to calm my nerves. I couldn't make any weather here. I couldn't hurt any human. Halfway to the car, I stopped.

Sasha.

Shouldn't I try to help him now? Shouldn't I try to save him now? I had my bag back. I finally had my phone with me. I could call someone for help. I might be able to make it.

As if reading my mind, Brigid said, "If she tries to call anyone, you have my permission to hit her."

Of course Brigid wouldn't let anything pass by her. But then Sasha was suffering... Everyone was watching me.

I had made my choice.

Without giving him a final glance, I turned my back on him and got into the passenger seat. I couldn't bear to face him anymore. I felt like I had betrayed him. No, I *had* betrayed him. I'd thrown him away. I sacrificed him. My heart filled with guilt as the car drove away.

During the drive, I kept looking at my phone, which was now turned on. I willed it to ring. But that didn't happen. Wasn't Maria curious as to why we were taking so long? Wasn't Arnold worried about my whereabouts? But I shouldn't blame them. I could've helped him. I had a chance. But I didn't take it. That was my choice. This was entirely my fault.

We arrived at my house. I wasn't surprised that Brigid knew where I lived, like how I knew where she lived. The driver looked disappointed that he hadn't had a chance to hit me. I think I would've retaliated if he'd tried to. He should have been grateful that I didn't try to hurt him.

I got out of the car and slammed the door. The front door opened, revealing Maria. Her smile quickly turned into a frown. The car reversed and left. Maria walked towards me.

"What just happened? Where's Sasha?"

"I left him with Brigid."

CHAPTER EIGHTEEN

I had called Arnold to rush back to school. But it was too late. Arnold said they were gone.

When he came home, I told them everything. Maria looked like she was going to cry and Arnold looked extremely angry.

"We have to help him. We can't leave him like that," Arnold said and stood up quickly.

"It's no use. We don't know where they are," I told him.

Arnold sat down slowly.

"Let's give him another call and see if he's alright." Maria took her phone out and called him. She left it on speaker and we listened to the ringtone, waiting for him to pick up. In the end, we were sent to voicemail for the hundredth time.

I shook my head. "There is nothing we can do for him now. For us to be safe, we have to leave him."

We sat there feeling helpless.

"When Brigid gave us that choice, I was sure he was going to choose himself. Why didn't he?"

I honestly thought he was going to choose to save himself. Instead, I was the one who chose to save myself. Because that would be what anyone would have done. That would be what any human would have done. I mean, don't all humans choose to save themselves? I didn't think he would...

"He's trying to change. And..." Maria said softly. "He loves you."

I ignored the latter, but I knew he was trying to change. I thought of the times he'd helped me. Again and again. He'd been proving that he was changing. That he was trying to be better.

"Am I being any different to the Old Man?"

When I said that, they both sat up straighter.

"Absolutely not."

"Dear..." Maria reached out and held my hand. "We all made our choices. Who could have known the outcome?"

"You did what you had to do to save our people."

"By torturing someone else."

I closed my eyes.

I wanted to help. I wanted to stand by his side. I wanted to fight back. But I couldn't without causing injury to myself resulting in a hailstorm. Without revealing my identity. Without ruining everything I had worked for. It could erase my existence if I hurt anyone. Even by accident. But what happens to me didn't matter.

It was Winterland that was more important. What would happen to Arnold and Maria if I was gone? What would happen to my people? What would the world become? How could I ever face my aunt?

"Layla... Please promise me."

But that was no excuse. I could have still done something. To leave someone like that... Especially someone who had helped me so many times. Where was my conscience?

I was the one thing I never wanted to be.

Helpless.

"You shouldn't think like that," Arnold said.

I opened my eyes. "I feel like a coward."

"Sweetheart." Maria squeezed my hand tighter. "He made his choice. You made yours. We wouldn't have expected any other choice from you. Could you imagine what would have happened if you'd risked it? Normally you would have taken the risk. For the first time, you didn't. You knew what the safer choice was, even when it was the hardest. You made the right choice this time."

Arnold came to our couch and sat on my other side and held my hand. Maria continued, "As long as you're safe. As long as you didn't get hurt. That's the most important thing to us. You have us. We're always on your side. You are nothing like him."

I held their hands tightly. To have two people who understand the choices I must make... To have them believe in me so much... What did I do to deserve them? As long as they were beside me, I could overcome any hard challenges. We were quiet, lost in our own thoughts.

To Maria and Arnold, I had made the right choice. To Sasha... I owed him a lifetime. I had to apologise. I should repay him. But at the same time, I didn't have the right to face him. If it were me, I would never forgive that person. Would he even want to talk to me ever again?

"I wonder if Sasha is okay now," Maria said.

"I know Sasha. He'll be fine. He'll find a way to keep himself well alive," Arnold said. "He was Brigid's second in command. I'm sure he'll find a way out."

I knew Arnold was trying to make us all less worried, but that didn't stop my overwhelming guilt. Something inside of me stirred. I sat up straight. My determination grew. I knew what I should do now.

* * *

I was sitting in chemistry class. We watched as the students started to file in. I glanced up whenever someone entered the classroom. He hadn't come for the past three days. Was he hurting? Was he injured badly?

Whenever I looked at Brigid, she seemed happy. Was she happy it had turned out this way? Was she glad he was hurt? The bell rang. He hadn't shown up today either.

I didn't see him or hear from him during the weekend. Each day Brigid got angrier as Sasha was still out of school – angry that her target hasn't returned. That she couldn't torment anyone. I was surprised she hadn't dragged him back.

That meant he was hiding very well. At least we knew for now Sasha was safe. But if Sasha was still injured, it was unreasonable for her to ask for him to come back to school already. Except she had always asked for the unreasonable. Always having it her way.

Then there was me, who was ungrateful. At times like these, he would normally get in contact with me. But he never texted me or called me. I was sure he was angry with me. I hadn't called him or messaged him.

I chose to keep silent because I was sure he'd never

want to speak with me ever again. But I should warn him about Brigid. I should tell him that despite his injury, he had to come back to school or else he'd suffer more than he already had. To think that he would have to suffer more... I didn't know if I wanted to tell him that either.

Arnold was worried that Brigid might turn her attention towards me again. But I reassured him that she couldn't. Or else she would break her word and she would look like a fool. But every day that passed, it looked like she would rather look like a fool than keep all her anger bottled up.

On the last day of the week, everyone at school was stressed. It was exam time. Not that it mattered to me, but I could see everyone was more tense than usual. Especially Brigid, but for a different reason. I knew she was at her limit because she was taking it out on the people who were around her. I avoided her like the plague. I knew this would be worse for Sasha once he came back.

We were sitting in chemistry while the students filed into class. Brigid locked eyes with me. I was sure she would storm up and unleash it all on me. But she moved towards an empty table and sat there fuming.

I glanced back at the door. *Sasha. You need to come in today. Or else you won't be able to bear the consequences.* Each person that walked in brought a little disappointment. When the bell rang to commence the start of the first class, any hope was dashed. I knew that whenever Sasha came back, whatever injury he received this time would be worse than any he already had.

CHAPTER NINETEEN

I came back from the river on Saturday morning, and I had decided. Today I would call or at least text Sasha. Ask if he was well. If he needed anything. To show my gratitude and to tell him I was sorry. I shouldn't have left it this long. No matter how guilty I was or how angry he was at me, I should have contacted him that same night.

Arnold had left to go training for the day and Maria was preparing breakfast. I looked at the time. It was only nine. Was this too early to call someone? I'd call him later then. I'd go and eat for now. I walked into the dining room as Maria sat down.

"Morning," she said.

"Morning."

"How was yesterday night?"

"Better than I expected."

She nodded at my answer and we dug into our droplet cakes.

We ate in comfortable silence. I was expecting Maria to say something. She hasn't been talking much lately. Nor had she been smiling or cheery. But every time I asked if there was something wrong, she would answer that she was fine. I had stopped questioning her. I knew why she was acting this way.

After breakfast, I went back to my room and stared at the phone. It was still too early to call. Maybe I should check on the paperwork with Maria and then call. So I took it, went back out to the dining room and started going through it with her.

By the time I finished, it was lunchtime. This would be the perfect time to call. He should be awake for lunch. But what if he was eating right now? I shouldn't disturb him if he was. So Maria and I ate in silence again. But when I looked at Maria, I knew she was ready to talk.

"Layla, you can do it."

Of course she knew. She knew what I was trying to do. She knew I was hesitating. I was surprised she hadn't mentioned Sasha since that day. She knew what I was thinking. How hard it was to say thank you. To apologise. She didn't want to rush or pressure me. That's why she left me alone… Left me to my own thoughts… My heart swelled with love for her. At times like these, she was the one who understood me the most. Like she was my own mother. That was probably why Arnold never mentioned Sasha, even if he had wanted to.

"Thank you." I just smiled at her.

After lunch, I went back to my room and stared at the phone. There could be no more excuses. I'd been following the same pattern for the past two weeks. I had to stop postponing. I should call him. I picked up the phone. My heart beating fast. My mind completely empty. I had to stop feeling guilty. I shouldn't hesitate anymore. I was about to press dial when suddenly the screen lit up with a call.

Sasha Reynold.

The phone was vibrating with his name on it. I couldn't believe what I was seeing. I was so shocked that the call eventually ended. I snapped out of it. And noticed that my room was colder than it was supposed to be. I shook off the initial shock. He called me again. I answered it right away.

"Hello?"

"Hey."

There was an awkward silence. But then I realised he was waiting for me to say something.

"Is there something wrong?"

"I'm in front of your house."

I froze. Then I stood up and walked out of my room. I didn't say anything. And he didn't say anything either. The only sound was my footsteps.

"Layla, where are you…" I passed Maria who was in the dining area and carried on to the front door. I opened it with one hand.

Sasha was standing there with the phone on his ear. Looking well. Looking healthy. He hung up and put the phone down. I did the same.

I couldn't believe it. He was here. He was standing right in front of me. No bandages. No crutches. No casts. A few scratches and bruises, but other than that he looked like his normal self.

"Why are you here?"

"Should I go home?" he joked, but when I didn't respond he turned serious. "I thought I should visit. I know how worried you might have been."

"But don't you hate me?"

"I understand why you did it. You just wanted to protect yourself."

Something came over me. I dropped to the floor and leaned my back on the wall. I pulled my legs to me and rested my head on my knees. Thank goodness he was okay. I'd known he was safe, but to see him alive and well… I never knew how worried I was until I saw him.

Sasha came into the house and closed the door. He stood next to me and started patting my head. I kept resting my head on my knees, but I was watching him.

How could he be so calm about this? I'd basically abandoned him. I was the worst. If it was me, I would never forgive someone who betrayed me. I would hate that person. Curse them till the day they died. He said that he understood, but how could he? Just that simple? He didn't have any memories of the time he caught me at the beach. So how could he accept that so easily?

I felt even more guilty now. I should have contacted him. I should have given him help if he needed it. I should have done something for him. I owed him that much. He kept patting my head as if to reassure me that everything was okay. We stayed like this for a couple of minutes.

"I'm sorry," I said.

"Apology accepted."

"Thank you."

"Gratitude received."

"No you don't understand. I'm–"

All of a sudden, Sasha bent down, grabbed my hands and pulled me up from the floor. He drew me towards him and hugged me. I stood frozen stiff.

"It's alright. Everything is alright now."

His arms were strong yet comforting. He smelled

like citrus and sandalwood. I slowly stepped back from his embrace. "You know that nothing is fine right now."

When we made eye contact, he knew that I was right. He knew he'd have to face consequences once he went back to school. He knew that Brigid was waiting for him. A quiet rumble filled the hallway. It was coming from Sasha's stomach.

"You haven't had lunch yet?"

"Or breakfast."

I walked to the dining room with Sasha following me. Maria was sitting there humming a happy tune. She must have seen our exchange. I wanted to tell her that it meant nothing, but at the same time I was happy that her mood was back up again.

"Mum, Sasha came over."

As if she didn't know already. But I told her anyway. Maria bounced over and hugged him. He hugged her back. He flinched a little and hid it well, but I caught it. How bad was his injury? Sasha looked over at me but I glanced away.

"I'm so glad that you came over! It's good to see you again." She held his shoulders as she looked at him. "Are you hungry? Do you want anything in particular?"

"Anything is fine."

"Something that's good for him," I said.

I think Maria got the message because she let go of

his shoulder and rushed out of the room. Sasha gave me a questioning look. I just shrugged. I also didn't know what was happening. Two seconds later, Maria appeared with a bag in hand.

"I'll be right back! I'm buying ingredients!"

Not that kind of message! Before I could stop her, she was out the door. The house was silent again. I internally sighed. Of course she would want me to be alone with him. And since I was at home and as long as I stayed away from the water, my secret wouldn't be found out again.

"I think she forgot that you're hungry right now. But have a seat. I'll check if the pantry has anything." I started to walk to the kitchen when Sasha stopped in front of me.

"Are you sure you're going to be okay?" He was thinking about my fear of water.

"I'll be fine. Mum is normally very careful with water so that I won't faint. I'm just looking for snacks for you to eat while we wait for her."

Sasha nodded, his warm brown eyes boring down into mine. I didn't know what to make of it and went inside.

This was such a strange place for me to be in. But it would be even stranger if Sasha went through our cupboards and noticed that they were fairly empty since we didn't normally eat anything except for droplets. I stared at the equipment and shelves. I'd never really been into this part of the house, since I never had a reason to. Plus Maria never wanted me to be in here anyway. So everything was unfamiliar to me.

"Do you want help?" Sasha called out.

"Stay there!" I yelled back.

I checked the top shelf, and as expected there was nothing. I tried looking near the condiments. There were cereal boxes. Why would we have cereal boxes? It made no sense to me why we would have any. Did Maria hope Sasha would sleep over one day?

I grabbed a box and shook it. There was half a box full. Should I give this to him? I looked at the box again. But it's *cereal*. Even I knew what cereal was meant for. I tried the other shelves with no luck. If he was really hungry... and Maria would take a while... I shook the box again. It was better than nothing right? I went out of the pantry and placed the box right in front of Sasha.

"Before you say anything–" Sasha started laughing.

I knew he was going to react this way. He gasped and grabbed his injured side, but he kept laughing anyway.

"Did I come at the wrong time?" He kept laughing as I stared at him.

For once, I didn't mind him laughing at me. Just watching him laugh right now made me feel... at ease. Like everything *was* alright. I started giggling and then

I laughed with him. It felt like everything was normal. I didn't want to admit this, but I was glad to see him again. That he was fine. That he was able to laugh.

"If you're not going to eat it, then I'll put it back," I said. I went to pick up the box when he grabbed my wrist.

"You found a snack for me, so I should try it."

I just shook my head and sat down next to him. He opened the box and put a handful in his mouth. "It's delicious."

"That's just your luck, Black Cat."

He raised his eyebrows. "Have I earned myself a nickname, Puddles?"

I smiled and rolled my eyes. But then I thought of his injury. "So how have you really been?"

He shrugged. "It's not as bad as you think."

I raised an eyebrow.

"Okay, it's bad, but I've had worse. At least I didn't end up in the hospital this time." Meaning he'd been in the hospital multiple times before. I stared at the floor.

"What happened… after I left?" I looked at him again. He had finished the cereal already and set the box on the table.

"She moved me to another place. The secret hideout, which I knew of. She kept threatening me along the drive, which I found funny. When we arrived I met a few familiar faces that wanted to… talk to me. She must have been disappointed that I didn't try to call anyone to help me, so she let me off, thinking that was the best punishment for me. After she left, it took me a while to get back home. But other than that, here I am. It doesn't sound so bad, right? So don't worry about it."

When he said it like that, I just felt even more guilty. The blood. And the pain. That wasn't something that I'd experienced. It must have hurt. With every breath that he had. And he had to endure it. All by himself. He didn't mean to make me feel bad – he only answered because I asked – but it made me feel fresh guilt all over again.

"How could you say that it wasn't bad?"

"Don't worry about it."

"How could you forgive me? Aren't you angry at me?"

"I'm not gonna lie and say that I wasn't. But I understand. No one wants to get hurt. If you could be fine, why wouldn't you?"

"Then why did you choose to get hurt?"

"Don't you know why?"

I didn't reply. I didn't know how to reply. But then he said, "We're friends. That's what a friend should do."

"I'm really sorry."

"But really, I felt like I owed you. I'm sorry that I started it. What you had to go through because of me. And then you got involved because you were with me. You didn't deserve that, since you're no longer Brigid's target."

He might have thought that way. But if I was to be honest, he had repaid me. Since the day when those boys came to the bus stop. He didn't owe me anything anymore. Instead, now I owed him.

"You know, I wondered why you never called me," he said.

"I didn't know what to say. Plus, I thought you were angry with me."

"I thought you didn't want to be friends anymore. Well, that makes me feel better."

"I was going to call today."

"I should've waited then."

Then I realised his face was so close to mine. But at that moment the front door swung open. We jumped apart at the sound.

"Give me ten minutes. I'll cook something–" Maria stared at the box on the table. "What's that? Cereal? Don't tell me you gave him *cereal*?"

Sasha started laughing all over again.

"He was hungry!"

"But cereal?!"

"There was nothing else!"

"You're not allowed in the kitchen!" Maria looked worried. As if my secret was out.

I shook my head. "Nothing happened."

She stared at me and I just nodded to reassure her. Sasha didn't know what was going on and just kept laughing. She calmed down and went straight to the kitchen.

"Give me ten minutes and I'll serve something."

I stood up. He grabbed my arm. I looked back at him.

"Where are you going?"

"To the dining table."

"Is she really going to finish in ten minutes?"

"Yes, she will."

We sat down and when ten minutes was up, she really did come out of the kitchen with a bowl of porridge for Sasha.

"Thank you."

"Start with this."

"*Start* with this?" Sasha exclaimed. Maria had already gone back to the kitchen. I smiled.

"And then finish the *rest*," I answered him when he looked at me. He just sighed.

No matter how many dishes and bowls came to the table, he ate them all. But then all the food was light and small. So it would be easy for him to eat. At least the dishes were good for his health. When he finished the last bowl, I couldn't help but feel relieved. He still had an appetite. Maria was cheering on the side. He looked like he needed a break from all the food he was having.

"Was that lunch or dinner?" he asked.

"Both," I answered.

"Haha. Funny." He smiled. Maria was just beaming.

"Okay you kids, go watch a movie while I clean this up."

"Thanks, Mum." She smiled and winked at me. I gave her a glare and she rushed to the kitchen. Thankfully, Sasha didn't see our exchange.

We went back to the living room where Sasha sat on the couch. I flicked through his case which he had forgotten and left here, but I didn't know what to pick, so I randomly chose a cartoon since it was safer to watch. But neither of us watched the movie. We were just staring at the screen. There was a lot I still wanted to tell him, so I spoke up first.

"Brigid is really angry."

He was quiet for a while and then said, "I know."

Of course he did. "Do you have any plans?"

"Nope."

I turned towards him. "But you're still injured. You shouldn't get hurt again so soon. You might not be able to recover."

"If that's the only way for her to be happy again, then that's what could happen."

No, that wasn't true. I was sure we both thought of

the same solution, but of course he wouldn't bring it up.

"I'll help you."

He turned and stared at me. "Are you serious?"

"I am."

He shook his head and turned back to the screen. "You shouldn't involve yourself."

"I already am. She could hurt me in the future if she ever changed her mind, so I'm already involved, whether I like it or not." I looked at him until he looked at me. "So why don't we bring Brigid down?"

We didn't say anything as the movie kept playing in the background. I should have brought down Brigid from the very beginning. If I didn't have so much at risk, I would have stood up to her then. But I had avoided this problem for far too long. All because I wanted my time in the human world to be as peaceful as it could possibly be before the true battle happened. I had not wanted any more trouble on my plate. But now, I was tired of hiding.

It was time to act.

This would be good for both of us. He could stop his suffering and Brigid would no longer be a threat to me. It would eliminate all future problems if we destroyed her position. It would be difficult. But it wasn't impossible.

"It'll be hard." He acknowledged my thoughts.

"I know, but we can do it if we work together."

He was silent but then he said, "I thought you didn't trust me?"

It was my turn to be quiet. I thought for a while, but then I responded, "Without me knowing, I've come to trust you."

After what we'd gone through together, how could I not? I subconsciously let my guard down the day when he chose to cooperate and lose his memory. From the time when he told Arnold that I was in danger at the bus stop till now when he chose to sacrifice himself. I had started to slowly trust him without me wanting it to happen. He was trying to change. And he was changing. And if he was changing for the better, why shouldn't I start to trust him?

Sasha smiled. "Alright, let's work together. Do you have a plan?"

"I've thought of something."

* * *

As soon as Sasha left to go home, Arnold came back from his training.

"Was that Sasha just now?" he asked as he entered the living room. I nodded. "He seems well. That's good." Even though his words were indifferent, I could hear the relief in his voice.

Maria also came in. "But you would not guess what

I heard! Layla is working with Sasha to eliminate Brigid and her group."

Arnold's eyes widened. "We are?!"

"We have to, or else I'm going to get hurt eventually. You know what happened before. It could happen again."

Arnold nodded. "But I thought you didn't trust him." When I didn't answer right away, Arnold said, "Or you didn't want to trust him."

"Now she definitely trusts him!" Maria said.

I didn't say anything because I didn't want to admit that they'd been right from the beginning, but they took my silence as an answer anyway and started cheering. I ignored them but couldn't help and smiled.

After they finally calmed down, Arnold asked, "We can go to the other plan now?"

"We have to focus on Brigid right now. She's our main obstacle at the moment. The Ministers haven't been giving us a hard time lately, so we can work on them later. After all, we still have a year. So after we get rid of Brigid, we can talk about other plans." Maria and Arnold exchanged a look I knew. They were clearly happy with where this was going. "No promises."

"Yes, no promises," Maria confirmed.

The next day Sasha came over for dinner. Maria served a variety of food as always. We ate at the dining table, discussing our plans. By the end of the meal, we all knew what our roles would be. As usual, we started clearing the table. Then, as always, Maria dragged Arnold into the kitchen to help her clean, leaving me and Sasha alone.

"What do you want to do now?"

"Let's go for a drive."

"No."

"I promise that it'll be safe. There's nothing to worry about."

"No risks."

Then Arnold stepped out of the kitchen.

"There is no–"

"That's fine!" Maria pulled Arnold back into the kitchen. "As long as she comes back in an hour, then be safe and have fun!"

I was going to disagree, but Sasha took my hand and walked me towards the front door. Something told me that he and Maria had planned this together.

"If she doesn't come back, I'll–" We never got to hear the rest of what Arnold said as Sasha closed the door.

"He's a worrier, isn't he?" Sasha said.

I took my hands from him.

"Because he cares about my safety."

"It's a place where there is no water."

"Doesn't mean it can't be dangerous."

"Everywhere is a risk. Even your place."

"It's safer than everywhere else."

"Where we're going is just like your home. Safe. Trust me."

I kept silent. I knew I had begun to trust him, but this was a completely different trust.

"Don't worry, I'll protect you."

After a long silence, I said, "If I think it's not safe, I'm not getting out of the car."

"Deal."

Since he was insisting, I decided I might as well go along. I was slightly curious. As we got to his car, he opened the passenger door for me. When he got in on the driver's side, I asked, "Where exactly are we going?"

"You'll see."

"I don't like surprises."

"You'll like this one."

He started the engine and reversed out of the driveway. We passed a lot of houses, but I knew we were heading south. I was not getting out of the car. There was no way I was going to risk revealing my identity or hurting myself. But then I noticed a familiar car behind us.

When I really looked at it, I saw that it was Maria's

car. I smiled. Of course they wouldn't want to risk it either. It must be Arnold in the car as I couldn't sense him. Sasha hadn't noticed but then he wasn't familiar with Maria's car. I relaxed. At least if anything happened, Arnold would be there. So I tried to find some clues.

"Stop trying to figure out where we're going."

"I can't help it."

"You won't figure it out anyway."

"How would you know that?"

"I just know you won't if you don't close your eyes soon."

I looked at him confused.

"We're heading towards the river. You might not want to see the water."

"I'm fine at night. Because I don't see the water clearly as long as I don't get too close to it."

"Interesting. But you didn't even know we were heading towards the river. So you do have a bad sense of direction."

He was right, but I didn't acknowledge that. "We're not going *to* the river right?"

"Of course not! What do you think I'm trying to do? Kill you?"

"I don't know. Maybe you're planning a kidnap right now."

"Let's commit the perfect crime. I'll steal your heart

and you'll steal mine."

I sighed. "Don't you get tired of saying these lines?"

We drove in a zigzag up a hill. I was slowly getting worried since it was quite dark until I saw the view.

"Wow, it's so beautiful!"

Sasha parked the car and we got out. We were on top of the hill, where we could see the city below all lit up. I couldn't help but get out of the car and see it properly. To be as close to the view as possible.

"I told you that you'd like it."

I ignored him and stared. It was beautiful. The lights in the city were sparkling like the stars above us. There were moving lights too – car headlights and taillights – so it looked like slow shooting stars on land.

With the wind blowing gently and the sounds of the city, it felt hopeful... peaceful. There is light in the darkness. It was a comforting thought. Then I heard music. I looked over at Sasha, who was wearing a blazer and had his phone out. It was a song used for ballroom dancing.

"May I have this dance?"

"I didn't think you liked to dance this much."

I tried to look for Maria's car. I couldn't see it, but I knew it must be nearby. Arnold was good at hiding. And that might have been better since I wouldn't want him to see me dancing with Sasha. This was slightly odd.

Sasha was waiting for my hand. And the music kept playing. It was the perfect mood and setting for a dance. So I took his hand and he drew me in. He led me in a small circle near the car, with the city lights shining below us.

"So why did you want to bring me here?"

"The next few days are going to be hard for us so I thought I'd bring you out to enjoy a little scenery before this all changes."

That was true. During the next few days, we would have to be cautious. Always planning and replanning our every move. We wouldn't have time for laughing or having fun.

"Plus, I wanted to enjoy what it would be like if we went to the ball together."

"Mum wanted to see me in a ball gown and have my picture taken. And Arnold wanted me to make more good memories. Or else I wouldn't have bothered to go through all the effort."

"No wonder you didn't give me an answer when I asked."

There was only one question to which he could be referring. And to be honest, I thought I might have the answer this time.

"I wouldn't have minded going with you."

Sasha stared at me. I felt slightly embarrassed.

"As a *friend*."

That was saying so much more than I wanted to say. It felt like I was saying more than I meant. But in truth, I wouldn't have minded going with him to the ball. It would have been... fun. It must have been the view and the music. I was telling him things I never thought I would say to him. I was being very honest with him at this moment.

"Of course as a friend."

"*Just* a friend."

"Nothing more." It sounded more like a question instead of a statement.

"Yes, a friend."

"You've mentioned friends many times. Or are you trying to convince yourself otherwise?"

"I'll stop being friends with you right now if you don't stop this."

"Stop what?"

I glared at him and he laughed. "But thank you for being my friend."

I stopped glaring at him and listened to the music as we continued to dance around the car. I looked out into the city lights. It was a beautiful sight.

"I'm... glad to be here in this moment with you."

I said it without much thought. I definitely was not grateful for all the trouble we'd encountered. Especially with my life, as well as Maria's and Arnold's, at stake. But it was these small moments when I could forget all the responsibilities that I had and the plans that I carefully made. When I could forget about all my worries. When I could forget the bad memories and live a normal life. I could just be... Layla.

There were moments in our struggle that had been fun. And it was thanks to Maria and Arnold but mostly it was also thanks to him. I hadn't been able to relax or enjoy myself like this since... Just the thought saddened me, and I quickly thought of something else. I couldn't let it rain. But moments like these were rare. He made me realise that I could enjoy life even when there were obstacles, as long as I had the most important people next to me.

Sasha smiled and gave me a wink. "I know."

I rolled my eyes. Looking at the city below, made me wonder how big the world was but also how small it was. Amongst the thousands of people who lived here, we'd still met. Amongst the thousands of lights, I was here sharing this memory with him.

"Life without you would be like a broken pencil..." I looked back at him. He was staring into my eyes. "Just pointless."

I sighed and stepped out of his hold.

"We should go. My curfew is soon."

"Okay, let's go."

We got back into the car and Sasha drove me home. We didn't say anything to each other along the way. It was a nice drive with a comfortable silence that had formed between us. Maria's car also appeared and followed us. I hoped Arnold hadn't seen or heard anything that happened. That would be too awkward.

When we pulled into my driveway, Sasha spoke. "I'll see you tomorrow."

Although he was giving me his usual smile and being his normal self, I could tell that he was nervous. Like he had a lot on his mind. I patted his head. He looked at me, stunned. I had only ever comforted Arnold that way. It was my first time trying to comfort him. I smiled awkwardly to reassure him. He kept staring at me. It looked like he wanted to say something else, but then he shook his head and sighed while I got out of the car.

"See you."

CHAPTER TWENTY

"I have a bad feeling about this."

Arnold was driving us to school. Today was the day that Sasha would start our plan. But it was also the day he finally returned to school after the fight with Brigid. She wouldn't miss the opportunity to make Sasha's life a thousand times harder than usual.

"We'll be fine."

"Maybe Sasha was right. Maybe you should stay at home so that you won't be involved."

"I won't be."

"But you might be. Like last time. But this time with an audience. It's safer to stay at home."

"On the first day of our plan, we should be present.

Because you never know what could happen, so we should be there."

"What if she hurts you?" Arnold whispered.

I knew he was very worried. I knew that Brigid could hurt me and everything could go wrong. But it was a risk I was willing to take if it meant that things would start to change from now on.

"I have you. And I also have Sasha. Everything will be alright."

Arnold sighed and nodded. "But whatever happens, I'll be right by your side."

I patted his shoulder. "Thanks Arnold."

He just smiled at me and parked the car.

We arrived later than usual. This was when most students would be at school. This was when Brigid liked to shine the most. We walked to our lockers. As soon as we opened the door to the hallway, we saw a couple of people heading towards a certain locker area. Arnold and I looked at each other. It could only mean one thing.

Brigid was already creating a commotion.

There was a large crowd surrounding Sasha and Brigid. Sasha looked defiant and Brigid looked like she was waiting for an answer. The group must have sensed my presence – or maybe they were waiting for me – because the audience created a pathway when I appeared.

I could feel everyone's stunned silence. Arnold was

still. My senses told me to run. That something was wrong. But I chose to help Sasha. I chose to be his friend. I refused to run away again. If we needed to, we'd go forward with the plan now, and then I would follow through. I stood where I was and Brigid saw me.

"Ah, the main character is here." Brigid was beaming. Sasha just closed his eyes – like he was defeated. Why was Sasha looking like that? What did she mean? Was she waiting for me? "I'm surprised you didn't run away."

"You wanted to see me?"

"No, no. We were just mentioning you. And for you to show up, it's the most perfect timing. Did you want to confess something?"

Confess? Did she know our plans already? We couldn't lose just yet. We hadn't even started. I tried to think through our options.

"Leave Sasha alone."

Everyone in the audience gasped. Even Arnold tensed beside me and Sasha looked at me. If she had somehow found out about the plan, it was better to be open and attack first, even if we lost our element of surprise. Though I had hoped we would have gone with the original plan since it was the better plan. But there was no turning back.

I had expected Brigid to get angry or even just stare at me in disbelief. That was how the Brigid I knew would always react. What I did not expect was for her to just laugh. "I guess I must have been right. You do like Sasha. *Puddles.*"

I stood very still. The word echoed in my mind.

Puddles.

Did I hear that correctly? My mind slowly processed what my ears had heard. I didn't laugh. I didn't move. I looked over at Sasha, who had his head down. It was something only between us. Something I hadn't even told Arnold. How could Brigid know... Unless...

"See how concerned she was for you!" Brigid then giggled and said, her tone high-pitched, "*Leave Sasha alone.*"

Then she turned back to her mocking voice. "As if she'd be able to protect you. She *does* have feelings for you. I mean, why else would you have gone to the ball with Sasha if he had asked."

There could only be one reason...

Brigid continued, "And cereal for lunch? What a joke! Calling him a black cat isn't nice, you know. And patting his head to comfort him! How endearing." She clapped her hands together, put them against her cheek and squirmed like she genuinely found it sweet.

But it couldn't be...

She looked at my face. She dropped her hands and folded them in front of her. "The disbelief on her face!

Why Sasha, you did a marvellous job. She fell for you *hard*." She started walking to me. "I always had faith in your charms, but I couldn't believe it. Layla is like an ice block. Who would have known you would be able to melt her heart?"

No, he did not. This could not be happening. That was when I finally looked over at Sasha, who was smirking at me.

"I told you she was a tough one, but that I'd be able to charm her anyway."

I closed my eyes. And that was when I knew.

I *knew*.

I shouldn't have trusted him. I should *never* have trusted a human. I should have known better. Humans would always betray.

I fell right into their trap. I thought he had changed. That he'd changed for the better. But no. They had planned this. Right from the start. Right from when Sasha defended me and got drenched in water. When Sasha started riding the bus. When he came to my house. When he must have organised the boys to come to the bus stop. When he offered to drive me home. When he hinted at a confession. When Brigid came to the bus stop. Yesterday night.

Everything.

Everything was planned. Everything for this

moment. To humiliate me. I'd thought she no longer paid me any attention. I was wrong.

"What a show we've put on," she said. "It was worth all the effort! I certainly enjoyed it. I really didn't think we'd be able to make her fall for it, but she did. Great job everybody! Especially you Sasha. You certainly did most of the work. And what an amazing result."

Brigid's gang clapped first, which encouraged everyone else to start clapping, and she laughed. Brigid was smiling, enjoying this. She curtsied in every direction. I had always thought Brigid would find a way to get her revenge. But I never expected Sasha to be getting his revenge too.

I should never have given him a chance. Should have never let my guard down. This display wasn't only her revenge, it showed she was undefeatable. That no one could escape from her. That she would always win, no matter what. A fine example had been made out of me. And it was a warning to everyone who was watching.

I didn't say a word. I couldn't say a word. They'd set me up to look as if I was infatuated with Sasha. Even though we both knew that wasn't the case. What they'd revealed and what I'd said had not helped with my case. Silence had always been my best weapon. Because I wouldn't want my words to turn against me. How ironic. Now I couldn't defend myself. There was nothing to protect me. No words could save me now.

But this wasn't the end yet. I had to finish this game. Brigid wanted to humiliate me. I would give her that. But I wouldn't let her get to me. And it was better to focus on Brigid than to think of Sasha.

Because every time my mind started to wander back to past events, to all the foolish decisions that I'd made, to all the hints I should have seen, I wanted to scream at the top of my lungs – letting all the emotion out. I could not believe how naïve I was to trust a human. But I needed to keep calm. I had to stay calm. I couldn't lose control of my emotions.

"She got played!" they whispered.

"How humiliating..." another whispered.

"Basically got rejected," one whispered.

"More like thrown away," said another.

"She was another name on his list of conquests then?"

The sound of thunder roared nearby. It was a miracle that a thunderstorm was forecasted for tonight. Arnold held my hand. I closed my eyes and tried to calm my nerves.

Don't let it get to you.

Don't feel anything.

Don't let them win.

It's not worth it.

The thunder slowly faded into the distance. I tried

so hard to control my feelings. All the years spent controlling my emotions had finally paid off. I wouldn't let this small matter ruin the bigger picture. I could do this. No matter how hurt I was. No matter how angry I was at myself. I could control this. I could endure this.

"You should be really proud of yourself, Sasha. You really did charm her. I guess you won the bet. Now I'm sad." Brigid pouted as if she really was sad.

"But you won the other bet," said another gang member standing next to her.

Brigid looked at me and smirked.

"Yes, of course you're right! How could I forget? She hasn't cried yet."

I just stared at her while Arnold held my hand even tighter.

"Sasha, you didn't make her break into tears even when she found out the truth, so I win the other bet." She put her hands on her hips and tilted her head at Sasha. "You see if *I* can't make her cry, then how could *you* make her cry?"

"You're right," Sasha responded.

"That makes me feel a lot better. In a way, I'm glad she didn't cry because of you." Then she paused, crossed her arms and brought a hand to her chin. "But to be honest, I *did* want to see her cry. I have to admit I'm a tad disappointed." Then she looked at me and smiled. "Should we do something now to make her cry and beg for mercy?"

She wanted to see me cry? Now this was all starting to make more sense. The reason why they made this bet. I hadn't shed any tears the last time we had an audience. She thought Sasha would be able to do the job this time around. Did she really think a boy like Sasha would make a girl like me cry? I wanted to laugh at her. Whatever she wanted to do next, I would be able to handle it. I wouldn't give her that satisfaction. I'd make her lose interest in me. Once and for all. So that she would never disrupt my life again.

Brigid stared at me and frowned. "She looks like she's ready to fight me. I think we have to do our worst if we want to see her cry."

A few of the gang walked towards me. I took a step forward. *I'll be ready for her worst.*

"Wait."

Everyone stopped at Brigid's command. She saw the murderous intent in my eyes. And was not happy about it. Of course, she wouldn't be. She wanted her victims to cry for help and live in fear. And hated it when someone fought back. She knew she wasn't going to have her way with me.

But then she really looked at me and smirked. She walked up to me, close enough that only I could hear her say, "But I can see how hurt you are and you're just enduring. Well, that makes me happy. Now you know to never mess with me. Ever again."

Before I could say anything in return, she stepped back and spoke to the crowd. "Since I'm in such a good mood, I'll let you run off. And I'll let you enjoy your last few moments of freedom. I look forward to seeing you next year, my dear marked one."

I thought it would be over. I was ready to endure anything so that she would stop this. But she knew that was what I wanted. Keeping me as her marked victim would be the worst punishment for me.

Brigid laughed, flipped her hair and strutted off. Her gang followed right after her and the crowd slowly disbanded. But Sasha remained. He was staring at me, so I stared right back at him. We stood there watching each other as Brigid walked away, laughing. Then there was silence in the empty hallway, but we continued to stare at each other.

Out in the distance, people were sitting around chatting, playing basketball or just walking to their lockers. But we kept staring at each other as if the world had stopped turning.

As time passed, it became harder for me to control my emotions. And the more I thought about it, the more foolish I knew I'd been. I should have seen the lies, well hidden under the truth. I should have never believed in a human. I should never have opened up to him to begin with.

This was why he kept persisting, wanting to be my friend and to spend time with me. It made no sense before, but now everything was clear. Every single movement, every single word.

No one had moved, but then Arnold launched himself towards Sasha.

"Arnold, go back to the car." I saw him tense, but he stopped. "Now."

His fists were clenched but he turned around and stormed out of the hallway. Sasha and I stared at each other for the longest moment again, his betrayal hanging in the air between us.

Then I pointed at him.

"Listen very closely, Sasha Reynold. The only reason why I was unable to detect anything was because you were able to mix the truth with lies. This will *never* happen again. Mark my words, I will make you regret this."

"Layla…"

He took a step forward. I lowered my arm and took a step back.

"Give me a chance to explain."

He took another step forward. I laughed. Did he

think he could play the same game? I gave him a glare filled with pure hatred and took another step back.

"Convince me."

He was going to take another step but stopped. I took another step back anyway. He knew there was nothing he could say to redeem himself. He knew that this was the end.

"I'm sorry."

With just two words, all the feelings that I'd kept in control... all the emotions I'd refused to feel were released. There was a mix of shock, sadness, and pain. But Brigid was wrong: I wasn't heartbroken.

I was enraged.

Angry at Brigid. Angry at Sasha. But mostly angry at myself. That I was a fool. I was so furious that – a single tear was shed.

In an instant, the sky turned from a bright blue to gloomy grey. Dark clouds formed. The air turned cold. I could feel it. Outside the hallway, everyone stopped what they were doing and stared at the sky. Little white flakes of ice fell from the sky.

"Oh my god!" someone said.

"Snow?!" another yelled.

"In summer?!" another exclaimed.

"But it never snows in Perth!"

Sasha was looking around at their reactions. Then

he looked at the snow that was fluttering to the ground. Then he stared at me. He was shocked, unable to utter a single word.

The silence between us was unbearable. I didn't want to face him any longer, so I turned around and walked away as he said,

"Forgive me."

To Be Continued

You can find Destarny at these places:

Website:
adestarnynovel.com

Twitter:
@adestarnynovel

Instagram:
@adestarnynovel

TikTok:
@adestarnynovel

Enjoyed the book? Support the author by purchasing a copy and leaving a review!

ACKNOWLEDGEMENT

A huge thank you to the Lethal Digital team who created such a beautiful logo for me.

A huge thank you to my editors, Lucy Rose York and Sue Copsey, who edited the book so that the story could become readable.

A huge thank to my cover designer, Steve Kuhn for putting up with all my requests to create such a beautiful book cover.

A huge thank you to the print on demand companies for printing my work and reaching it to a wider audience than I ever could.

A huge thank you to Lan who inspired me to write this story and for her endless advise, input and feedback.

A huge thank you to my mum who raised and took care of me. I don't know what I would do without you.

A huge thank you to Pia, Caroline and Josel who showed moral support and looked out for me.

A huge thank you to Matthew who gave endless support and encouragement whenever I needed it.

Lastly and most importantly, a massive thank you to my readers who are giving this story a chance and read it. I hope you enjoyed it!